T0106346

A Single Mother's Hu$tle

Ericka Blanding

authorHOUSE®

AuthorHouse™
1663 Liberty Drive
Bloomington, IN 47403
www.authorhouse.com
Phone: 1-800-839-8640

© 2011 Ericka Blanding. All rights reserved.

No part of this book may be reproduced, stored in a retrieval system, or
transmitted by any means without the written permission of the author.

First published by AuthorHouse 06/24/2011

ISBN: 978-1-4634-1423-8 (sc)
ISBN: 978-1-4634-1424-5 (e)
ISBN: 978-1-4634-1425-2 (hc)

Library of Congress Control Number: 2011909220

Printed in the United States of America

Cover picture done by: Lloyd Parks CEO of Goergous Magazing
Make-up done by: Milan Stapleton
Style List: Dazour aka ZourBella
Jewerly From The Royal Love Collection

Any people depicted in stock imagery provided by Thinkstock are models,
and such images are being used for illustrative purposes only.
Certain stock imagery © Thinkstock.

This book is printed on acid-free paper.

Because of the dynamic nature of the Internet, any web addresses or links contained in
this book may have changed since publication and may no longer be valid. The views
expressed in this work are solely those of the author and do not necessarily reflect the
views of the publisher, and the publisher hereby disclaims any responsibility for them.

Prologue

What have I done? My girls are being held by Roc, a nigga who tried to rape my friend, and to top it off my so- called other friend J helped him do it. Now I have to go and fight to get my girls back and my right hand bitch was being held hostage. When I finish with Roc and J, Shaya was next; no matter what, she's going to die. I know - I've hustled all my life and taken a couple of people's lives, but now it was my turn - or was it? As I stare down this long hall looking at the room that has my girls, my hearts ache for them. Are they dead are they alive? Did he touch them? But as I head toward the room I hear them.

"Chyna you a true female hustler it's in your blood". "Take no prisoners leave no one standing, we got you."

Joe, Auntie L and Mama Betty we all here. I knew they wouldn't let me down. I stuck my hands in my pocket checked my guns. I was ready. But wait, What the fuck?! I was so caught up that I never heard the door open behind me. My mouth was covered and my hands held behind my back. I was being dragged into another room.

So sit back and, Learn The Hu$tle.

A $ingle Mother Hu$tle......

Chapter One

Lesson One: Stand Your Ground Never Run

I was lying on the beach talking to a chick I had meet on the plane. She seem cool but all she talked about was Harlem. Harlem this, Harlem that - the way she talked you would've thought she was a tour guide for Harlem.

"So Chyna, how long you goin to hide out in ST. Tropez?"

"I told you Lady I'm not hiding, I'm living."

"You can't tell me you don't miss the heat and the streets".

"Can't say I do. Lady listen, I need to make a call. I'll chec you later."

Good she gone she was getting on my dam nerves with this Harlem shit. The more she talked about it the more I missed it - that's why I needed her to go. Look a here, Jay-Z n B on their yacht chilling. Do it B, you know chicks haten. I luv B and Hov the hood meets the glamorous life. That could be me and my king KK.

"Miss Chyna you have a call you can take it in the lounge area, thanks Mac."

"Hello who this?"

"It's your Aunt Pat, so how the good life treating you?"

"It's ok, well don't forget us back here. Never that. Aunt Pat you ok?"

"Yeah baby just checking in on you, ok we'll talk later."

My Aunt Pat been calling a lot lately something aint right. Maybe I should head home, I'd been here three months and was growing bored. Only the rich came though here. Fifty and the G Unit, Puffy, Hov all

1

the rappers. I had no interest in them and the only other men where white. Not my style. Let me call my girl.

"Hello can I speak to Mary?"

"Mary speaking." "Is it like that Mary?"

"You forgot your girl already?"

"Chyna is that you?"

"Please tell me you coming home, I can't take this replacement,"

"Replacement, they replace me?"

"No she a temp but I'm ready to kill her ass."

"Don't worry the boss is on her way back."

"Mary book me on the first flight tonight back to NY."

I heard Mary holla, yes the boss coming home, Chyna I'll call you right back with the flight information. Lady was back in her hotel feeding her boss info.

"KK how you upset with me and you got a girl,"

"Lady don't play is she ready to come home?"

"Not yet but I'm working on it."

"Lady hurry the fuck up I need her back in Harlem." "Got you."

How was I going to do that? I'll have to work on that later. Tonight I need to do me.

I need me some dick and quick.

Mary called. She had me on the 7pm flight arriving at 4am. I like that; no one would be checking for me. I would be free to move around. While I checked out the hotel.

I look for Lady to say goodbye but she was no where in site. I figured she had finally hooked up with Lloyd Banks. He'd been checking for her sense the party the other night and I guess being in the same hotel helped. Good for her. Get it, Lady. I jumped in my cab heading for the flight that would put me back into the belly of the beast. I wanted to surprise KK by calling and have him meet me but a female pick up his house phone.

"Nene?"

"No this Meka."

"Well Meka can I speak with KK?"

"Who this?"

"This Chyna,"

"Hey Chyna."

"It's me Meka from the mailroom."

"Ok Meka is KK there?"

"No he went to get us something to eat."

"That's you Meka?"

"Yeah I got me a Boss."

"Yeah you do, can you tell him I called."

"Thanks Chyna." "Meka what the fuck you doin on my phone?"

"It rung and I didn't see your help so I answered it."

"Who was it?" "It was Chyna, Chyna! "Yeah she said to tell you she called."

"Did she leave a number?" "No,"

"Meka let's get one thing straight - if you ever answer my phone without my permission I'll cut your tongue out your fucen mouth!"

"Now be up out my house!" "KK why you talking to me like that, all I did was take a call."

KK was Hot. Not only had Meka violated by answering his phone, Chyna called and he missed it. Where was Lady? He needed to check her ass quick. Lady was bent over the couch, ass up in the air with Lloyd Banks dogging it out.

"That's it nigga, kill this ass. Set it on fire." "I got you ma put your head down and open your legs wider." "There you go hit it papi don't stop that shit in deep. Lloyd was banging Lady; back out. Sweat was running down his chest his hands gripped her ass so she couldn't get lose. They where fucking like dogs in heat when Lady phone went off. She knew who it was immediately. 2Pac thug life came blasting out. Lady was too caught up in getting her back bent to stop she would just take her punishment like the warrior she was.

"Fuck she at?" It's ok, she'll get back and when she do I'll handle her ass."

When my flight landed my driver Bill was there.

"Hello boss, glad to see you home." "Glad to be home."

My first stop was to the locker my cousin people put the money bag in. I didn't know how much I was holding but the weight let me know it was large. Next I called my girl Mary. "Good morning boss lady." Good morning Mary."

"What you need?"

3

"I need you to call the team, and let them know meeting at 8am sharp."

"And what time does my replacement arrives?" "She get's here 6:30am."

I rode the rest of the way in silence. I was happy to be home back in charge, on top where I belonged.

"Your home Miss Whyte." "What time should I pick you up?" "Be back here at 6am."

I walked back up in my building, mama's home my door man George seem happy to.

"Hello Miss Chyna you where missed." "You too George."

"Good I'll have your bags brought up."

"No rush I'm going back out, see you later."

My key slid into the lock like water. My condo was cold there was no smell just coldness. I quickly changed that. I lit some brown sugar vanilla Bath n Body works candles. Soon my home was opening up to me. I hit the system and Anita belted out. My feet played toe tag with my deep plush carpet. I started my 8 head shower. New York in the spring was golden. Taking a shower in my home felt good. I really did miss being here, as I dried off it all came back to me. My aunt and cousin murder I needed to shake this shit off. My fam wouldn't want me to mourn them this way. I finshed lotioning off with my Dolce & Cabana The One. This perfume did something to me; it took over my body like a drug. I sported my Channel white linen suit, pink Channel tank top, and pink Ashley Steward thongs along with my Jimmy Chew 4inch pink sandals, pink Gucci bag pink diamonds stud and pink Gucci watch. Yes the boss chick was home now to get this wannabe the hell up out my office. I step up in the building, heels hitting the marble tile. My body was on fire. I love the smell of money. The American Express building had it on every floor but nothing like the top which I sat on. When I step off the elevator I looked for Miguel. No such luck, I'll deal with his ass later. There was my girl Mary with a clown smile plastered on her face.

"Good morning may I ask who are you?"

"I'm Lisa Whitfield, and you?" "Well first get your feet off my desk two you're a temp and last but not least pack your shit Lisa and get out of my office."

"You can't fire me." "Only Mr. Webler can."

"Bitch please, you got two seconds then you'll need security."

"Mary, call Mr. Webler." "No need I'm right here now you heard Miss Whyte remove your things from her office."

"Miss Whyte here's your tea and paper." "Thanks Mary now can you see Lisa out?" "Gladly." "Let's go she needs to speak with the boss."

"Welcome back, Miss Whyte I hope your time off was well spent." "I enjoyed it."

"Good, now that your back I can rest knowing the top boss is on her job."

"Mr. Welber, let's cut the bullshit."

"I'm back 100% and will give you the next money maker."

"Good because that bitch Lisa was getting on my last nerve with her no - talent ass."

"You a funny as white man but I still love you."

"I'll let you get settle in."

Yes, the boss bitch was back sitting here at my desk, it had my blood pumping, not to mention I was now ten million dollars richer due to mama plus extra my fam Auntie L and Joe left. The girl is back.

Chapter Two

That Nigga Black

"Miss thang you look good, can I holler at you a minute?"

"First, my name is not Miss Thang -it's Chyna. And no, you can't holler at me, you can speak. Now make it quick."

"Damn, Miss Chyna, I just wanted to take you out, maybe get to know you a little better, but you mean."

He made me smile. It had been a while sense a man made me smile. And that's how it started for Black and me. To say it was easy would be a lie. You see, Black was a hustler- at least that what he thought he was doing. Truth Black was lazy and even lazier when it came to hustling.

"Black, how come you always broke?" You stay out all night hustling as you call it then come up in here talking about it was slow, yet you manager to have a bag of piff with a new pair of sneakers." "That's my fuckin business, not yours. Stay in a chick place, this a man world. Remember that."

"Bitch you done lost that half of brain you got left. You not talking to them bitches on the street. My name is Chyna. This mine, not ours, so watch how you talk to me."

"You a real funny chick. You swear you hard body don't you?" "Whatever."

"Whatever? If I bring this steal, too that dome you wont talk that slick shit."

"It was my turn to laugh, Ha-ha -ha."

I knew this nigga was straight pussy. The sound on the street was out. I had to let him play hard. His dick and tongue game was vicious and at this moment I needed both. "Black, you know I love you, so why we hollering? Let's stop all this and get naked and do what we do best - putting dents in the wall."

I sexy walked over to him, stuck my hands between his legs, and ran my nails all over his big dick. He closed his eyez. I knew I had him. I bit down on his ear. He grabbed my fat ass and stuck his tongue down my throat. We played tongue games while we felt each other up.

"Chyna, take them clothes off." "You wanna watch?" "Without a doubt."

In the back round my nigga Jay was spitting them lines (I know what you like). My Vicki bra slid off my 44dd. They stood at attention, chocolate brown begging to be played with. I gently squeezed them, lifting both of them to my tongue, wetting both nipples at one time.

"Do that shit again, baby. That shit make my dick hard."

I did as I was instructed and sucked both nipples at one time. My free hand slid between my thighs landing on my big pink pearl pocking out. You see, I had the kind of body bitches prayed and paid for. I was 5'2, thick in the hips, a face that made blind men see and to say I had a big ass was a fucking lie I had the type of as that you seen coming even before I got there. Shit, J-Lo took a million out on that ass. If I had to put insurance on this ass I would need at least 10 mil a cheek and that's the truth. My body was hot chocolate from head to toe. My lips on my face and between my legs was vicious - both of them could get a hard nigga 'n bitch to part with all their worldly possession.

"Chyna, you taking to long with that thong."

"So why don't you put that tongue up in there and help me out?"

Black licked his lips, put his head up on the pillow and I spread my pretty pussy lips and landed on the only place it likes to sit: right on his face. Black wasted no time tonguing kissing my shit.

"Yeah that's right eat this pussy." My pussy was soaking wet. The way Black was eatin, all you heard throughout the room was sucking and slurping. Black ate my pussy as if his life depend on it and I let him.

"Ride this tongue bitch."

"You know you my bitch, Black."

I lost control I couldn't control my body I road his face like a cat in heat.

"Black I'm cumming, I'm cumming."

I grab that head, locked that tongue in position and cam all over that nigga face and down his throat. My legs shook, tits was on fire. I needed that third leg up in me deep. I climb of his face, bent over, spread my lips, and stuck one finger in it, telling him now make her do what it do (her being Susie -Q - that's my girl name) between my legs. My nigga got off the bed licking them pussy eaten lips, grab that 9 inch and started teasing my girl, sliding it up and down getting that dick real sticky. He slid that chocolate stick between my ass cheeks grinding up all on my ass. He was killing me.

"Black, stop fuckin around and ride this pussy right."

"You want this dick don't you?"

"Yeah nigga now slide it in this whole 'before I change my mind."

That woke his ass up quick. He grab my apple bottom ass an ran that dick up in me. He rock me a little. I looked back at him smiling. Black road my pussy like a man who rides his bike long and hard but a bitch like me was no slacker. I grab the head board and road back.

"Chyna, nobody has pussy like this - this shit make a nigga holler."

And holler he did every time I gave him any.

"Black, don't talk. spank this ass like I taught you."

With that said he pulled my hair with one hand, breast with the other, and punished my pussy walls in and out, up and down. This nigga was putting a hurting on me and I loved every bit of it. I had to hold onto the wall to keep my balance. Cum ran all down my inner thighs. Black fell back on the bed breathing hard and sweating. I just looked at him. If he put as much work in at hustling as he put in laying that dick I wouldn't come at him so much. I jumped in the shower to relax and clean the temple. One thing I learned from my mama: a clean pussy is the best pussy, period(**This one's on me ladies you never know when that pussy power maybe needed, so keep it clean**). I step out the shower remembering that slick shit Black shot at me about putting that gun to my head. One thing I learned from hustling is this: if a nigga or a bitch can speak it, than they can do it. I put my game face on, came up out the bathroom. He was sleeping in the spot I left him in. My steps was soft but deadly. I reached behind my head board and pulled out the whisper twins. Climbing up on the bed I sat on that man chest and, kissed his lips real hard. He woke up to two nickel plated 45s with silencer attached.

"What the fuck you doin boo?" is all he could whisper. I stuck one of the twins in his mouth, the other to his head. Speaking in an ice tone I said,

"If you ever threaten to put that heat to my head again I'll rock your punk ass to sleep,

do you feel me?"

Black looked at me and knew I was serious as a heart attack. He just moved his head up and down and with that he lived to see another day. Black knew from my history that my whisper twins was not to be played with and testing me could mean death. My guns was all I had left to hold me close to the only man that ever loved me and taught me everything I knew about hustling. That man was my cousin Joe. The name Joe rung bells all over Harlem. He was the man before his demise. My cousin was taken from me by the same lame ass nigga I was sent to kill. In the process they took my Auntie L. To this day I still hold there deaths personal and know that if anyone else beside Cha-Cha played a hand in it they where dead.

Chapter Three

Lesson Three: Never Sleep On A Nigga

As I climb off that nigga chest he kept his eyez on me and mine on him. My phone ringing broke our stares.

"Make it do what it do."

"Chyna, why you sound like that?" LaLa spit through the phone.

"This nigga Black, done step off a bridge, so I had to catch him."

"Let me holla at J we'll be there in 2. No it's good, that man leaving. I'll hit you when he disappear."

"Chyna, before you hang up, you got them by your side?" "

"Now you know me better than that, cool holla when he gone."

"Chyna that stunt you just pulled wasn't called for - that's why I stay out."

"You show a nigga no respect."

"Fuck respect. You spoke out of turn on me and I don't take that shit lightly."

"Fuck you C, I just ate that pussy right and bent that ass and still you bring that heat. I'm out. See you when I see you."

"Black I can care less where you're at but if you don't put that fête on the table I'm whisper real nasty at your back."

"Here's your fête. I'm out. I have to see a man name KK."

"KK? You talking about NeNe twin brother?"

"Yeah how you know that man?"

"Black please, everyone knows about the twins KK and NeNe."

They we're the shit on the west side. They had shit on smash nothing moved or sold unless them two gave the ok. If you got caught trying to move something, that was your life, and from what I heard it was done real nasty.

Nene girl Gemini found out first hand. NeNe was a pretty bitch but she love pussy as much as the next nigga and pussy stayed chasing her ass. She hooked up with this chick Gemini. Gemini was a model chick. She was 5'11, big titties, long legs, her skin was the color of honey. Her hair hung down to her ass. She had big lips, long eyelashes and blue eyez. Her and NeNe was goin at it hard. They rode around in that BMW 525XI black and no one touched or looked their way but Gemini was a little too greedy for her own good. Every time her girl went out of town or road with her brother Gemini would dip into both pots, the coke and money, supplying her man Chip with the goodies. They thought they had it made. When Nene and her brother found out her and KK planned Gemini and Chip's murder down to the R in murder. It was Thursday. Nene planned a romantic evening rose's, candles, food, the works.

"Nene, you my baby. No one can touch you boo."

"Is that right? Then show your girl."

Gemini stood totally nude and started rocking her hips, too SADE, (This Is No Ordinary Love). Gemini was feeling herself, popping her ass all up in Nene face.

"Like this boo, that's it ma, now get that Henny bottle and do that special thing you do with your pussy."

Gemini grab the Henny bottle, sat it on the edge of the table, then lowered her pussy on it and made the bottle dam there disappear. NeNe love this - this shit got her pussy wet. Watching Gemini fuck her favorite drink was her turn on.

"Faster baby, fuck my shit, faster go deep on it."

Gemini road that bottle like it was Chip's dick in her. NeNe phone rang - she knew who it was. It was part of the plan.

"What's good twin? You need me? Now. I'm on my way. I'm sorry baby I need to head out of town. My brother needs me. We'll finish this up when I get back on Sunday." "Ok baby hurry back home."

Gemini kissed NeNe goodbye and went to work on the stash, she copped two bricks of that powder then 20 thou in cash. She headed out the door jumped in her Mercedes. She was so hyped up on getting to Chip to surprise him with the gifts she just stole that she didn't even notice the Lexus creepen behind her. Gemini pulled up on 110th n Lenox running into the building. 5th floor apt 5-B Chip opened the door. She slipped in with that lust look in her eyez. Chip grab the bag, peeked in and a smile came across his face. Gemini dropped her mink, exposing her pure nakedness. Chip walked over to her, dropping the bag with the money and coke.

"You did good baby. We goin eat lovely of this."

Gemini started to say something but Chip started running his hands all over her body, slowly kissing her lips, tracing them with that wet tongue. Gemini dropped her head back, totally caught up. Chip put one tit in his mouth, milking it then the other one. Gemini moaned and quivered from the heat. Gemini pushed his head down she needed that pussy licked. Chip followed as he got on his knees. Gemini leaned up against the wall placed one leg on his shoulder. Chip held one ass cheek while his other had spread her lips into a V and went at that cat first flicking at her clit with the tip of his tongue then tickling it with the tip of his nose. Gemini grabbed that back of Chip head.

"Eat it nigga, don't play with it."

"Slow down baby I got this."

"Whatever my dude, I'm dick starved so eat it so I can ride that dick."

"Say no more let's move this to the bedroom."

When Gemini reached the bed she laid back, spread her legs wide. With her pussy exposed Chip licked his lips, ready for the sex marathon. Chip leaned in, licking her inner thighs. Gemini was feeling this. She squeezed on her tits, putting them in her mouth. She lapped at them as Chip ate that pussy just as Gemini closed her eyez to enjoy her tongue bath she heard a voice that almost made her heart stop.

"Don't stop, keep goin. She loves her pussy ate so please finish."

As Gemini opened her eyez, standing at the edge of the bed was NeNe and KK and their killer Lady. Lady was a bitch with no heart so Gemini knew what was next. As Chip lay between her legs he also knew he was about to die. He knew and heard of the twins;

Chip spoke first between the two. "

"NeNe, it's not what you think." KK swung.

"Nigga who you think you talking to? You laying with my sister chick that my sister fête on your table along with our product, what else could it be?"

Gemini laid on the bed watching Lady who was tapping the dresser.

"Gemini what's the matter? You're shit was just soaking wet now you all dry. Yo get back to eatin that pussy. I want her to get that last orgasm before the lights go out in this motherfucker."

"NeNe please, let's talk in the other room." "Fuck talking, eat that pussy nigga." NeNe snatched the machete from her pants. Chip went back to eatin Gemini pussy. Before he could get his chin wet NeNe took his head off, leaving it between Gemini legs. Gemini hollered but Lady was on her before she could finish. Lady stuck her nails in Gemini eyez. Blood ran all down Lady's hand. She smiled enjoying her kill. She pulled out with Gemini eyez stuck to her nails. Lady put Gemini eyez in a bag and handed them to her boss.

"Finish that bitch off Lady and be out."

"Got you."

When all was done Gemini laid with no eyez, nipples cut off, Chip's dick stuck in her mouth with his head chopped off laying between her legs. Everyone knew who did it, but nobody spoke on it. KK and NeNe was ruthless, plus they where teamed up. Their father was Columbian and their mother was Jamaican. They had the best of both worlds. Soon as Black hit the door I got my girls on the phone.

"Yo, LaLa spoke first. Do we need to dead that man?"

"No, I have a bigger problem." "What?" J hollered.

"I think I'm pregnant." "Pregnant!" "Don't everybody speak at once."

"Chyna what you goin do? I don't know." "I have to pee on the stick first before I can do anything." "We on our way. Have the answer when we get there."

I went in praying I wasn't bunned up. The last thing I needed was a baby, while I waited on the result mad shit ran threw my mind. What would I do? Would I have it or kill it? Black ass was always faken the last thing I needed was a baby by his fake, no hustling ass.

The bell rang. LaLa and J was all I had after Joe and Auntie L died and we straight banged out.

"So what's the verdict hoe?"

"I got your hoe bitch." We all laughed.

"Don't know yet. I waited on you two slow bitches so we can see at the same time." "Let's get it popping."

I pick up the stick off the vanity. We all stared in shock. Two pink lines nobody - spoke for a minute.

"Chyna what you goin do now?"

"Can't call it yet J, this shit fucked up." "What the fuck I'm goin to do with a baby?" "That's what you get for fuckin raw."

"You right about that one but we went to the doctor and the dick was disease free, plus that shit is pretty and you know I love the raw steal."

"Well let's get back to my baby."

"Your baby? Bitch the last time I check I was the one bunned up."

We fell out laughing but we all knew it wasn't funny.

"Let's go out. We'll decide later what's my next move."

"Your right." "Let me get dressed."

I opened up my walkin closet thinking, about my next move. I threw on my Baby Phat jeans, hugging my big ass with my white bustier, Baby Phat sandals and grabbed the clutch purse with my double RR keys, looked into the mirror and made up my mind I couldn't have this baby, not now. Me and the girls headed to the pier. It was hot and all the cars was out. Niggas lined up and down the pier. We came down the street shaken and snapping our heads to that nigga DMX Slipping Fallen. Heads turned. Niggas and bitches, the ones pushin, showed respect. The ones walking was haten' but they knew better. It was three the hard way ridin and getting your wig pushed back came with ease, fuckin with us. As we played the pier I thought back on how we ended up together. LaLa was a shy little something when I met her in Julia Richmond. She stayed to herself and this made her an easy target. One day I was headed to the gym when I heard stop I don't want this. I looked over into the back staircase and saw this big nigga Roc trying to stick his dick into LaLa's ass. She was trying to resist. She had no wins on that big nigga I crept up behind them and kick the shit out of Roc. He fell on LaLa almost crushing her. I kicked him again this time in his nuts. He screamed like a bitch and fell into a fetal position. I reached for LaLa, she was bleeding from her ass. She was really hurt. I told her to wash up in the bathroom sink and she would be ok with me. I wouldn't let no one fuck with her no more. I got Roc jump by my cousin Joe and his team. I lied and said he tried to kiss and touch on me. To say he got his ass whipped was a joke. My cousin and his team made a mark out of his ass.

Running with me made LaLa come up out that shy shit when she learned to rock with her hands or anything she could get her hands on. She was a beast. She beat bitches ass on GP and goin after me was a sure fire way of feeling LaLa's pain. That's how we teamed up with J. J was a bad chick. She had legs for days, small waist, nice breast, light coco complexion, and dreads that she kept tight. J was a sneaky bitch. She came into Julia Richmond with an attitude. Her mother made her transfer after her guidance counselor told her J was doing the basketball team star and his girl and her crew was looking to put their initials in her face. J walked in thinking her shit didn't stink. She walked up on LaLa.

"Yo where the office at?"

"First my name aint yo, and you skipped right past it."

J didn't like LaLa's tone. As she turned to leave J hit LaLa with her book bag. LaLa jumped up and grab J ponytail, jerking her back. Before LaLa seen it, J caught her with a mean right. LaLa didn't let that faze her; she was a champion with the hands. She swung back, connecting and dazing J, but J was mean with her hands too. Them girls fought like two cage animals, neither falling, too afraid of what people would say. As the crowd grew bigger entered Joe and I we noticed LaLa scrapping.

"Chyna. You turned that girl into a monster." "Like you did me?"

"You know we need to break this up."

We made our way over to the fight. I grab LaLa first Joe grab J. Big mistake.

J thought she was getting jump and sucker punched Joe. Bad move and everyone around her knew it. Before she could catch her breath I put her lights out. When she woke up she was in the nurse's office with a broken nose and two split lips. LaLa and I waited on her. As she came out of the office she noticed us. Winking in our direction we knew from there it was us three for life. When she got back to school she looked us up and the rest, as they say, is history. Now here we are 5 years later still riding hard. We played the pier for a while. I really wasn't paying anyone attention until the black Mercedes pulled up pimped out by Funk Flex. While it parked I watched it close; it was KK with wifey Meka. That bitch just made it cause had I stayed in town KK would be mine.

"What up Chyna?"

"Nothing Meka, what up with you?"

KK step up, "Meka you ready?" "Hello KK." "Hello Chyna."

"Meka let's go." As they walked KK peaked over his shoulder watchin my every step. "That nigga getting it and if Black play his hand right so will I."

"Black trying to get down with KK and NeNe?" "Yeah, let's pray he do."

The girls and I strolled a little while longer with my mind elsewhere.

"LaLa, J I'm out." "Where you goin? You our ride."

"Well catch a cab bitches. I'm tired. Plus I have a lot on my mind right now."

I kissed my girls goodnight, headed to my car and was out when I reached home.

There was note on the table I knew it was from Black. It Read:

Yeah ma I know this is a fucked up move but you left a nigga no choice. I can't bang with you no more you act like a nigga don't have no balls like you the man so I'm gone. I'm on a new team KK put me on so I'm teamed up proper. Here's your 10 thou you gave me to get in when I first started. See you when I see you.

P.S. I noticed the pregnancy test in the bathroom. Hope you do the right thing because don't know baby whole no nigga.

Chapter Four

Lesson Four: Things Never Turn Out the Way You Expect Them Too

"Baby girls get up. You two have to get ready for school."

"Ah ma it's to early." Baby Girl hollered.

"No it's not, Now get up before I make it do what it do." They laughed.

"Ma you're a mess trying to sound all hip."

"Please, your mother still got it."

My baby girls was a spitting image of their mother. They both where 5'6 big pretty eyez, bodies to die for and attitudes to go with it. I trained my girls from the gate, letting them know everything. From getting their periods to how to put on a condom, showing them that no nigga was worth their treasure if he couldn't do everything their mother and godmothers was already doin. My babies was spoiled from birth. They wore and sported nothing but the best. Prada, Gucci and LV coming out their asses. I spared no expense on my little girls. I did it because I love them and to let their dead beat farther know we didn't need his ass even though he was holding and because my mother Betty did it for me always.. Plus I wasn't 100% that he was their father. Sense linking up with KK and NeNe his paper was longer, not to mention he was pushing the Chevy Tao, all black, Fat Joe rims and a custom mad DUB system. When I first had the twins Lynda and Betty - yes that there real names - after my Auntie L and my mother Betty. I thought about getting back with him, but after a couple of late nights him not showing up for appointments. I knew to move on and I found out he had wifed some chick that ran with Meka. So I stepped up my game and took care of mine. I took my girls under my wings like I did LaLa and J, and just as Joe, Auntie L and my mother Betty did me. Them two where true hustlers. They sold candy in school that I got from Costco, when their designer bags and shoe's went out of style. They sold them to girls who couldn't afford them at retail price. No lam as niggas could fuck with my twins and chicks knew fuckin with one meant a double ass whuppin. That's the way they where taught.

Their godmothers and I schooled them on niggas spitting that pussy eatin game and that blue ball bullshit.

"Mommy you know this nigga?" "Watch your mouth Lil Mama."

"I'm sorry. You know this lam at our school, told me that my father ok it for him to wife me or my sister."

"What you say?" "I said nigga please, my mother is our father and she kill you first before she let you wife one of her baby girls."

"That's my girl." Stay two steps a head of these low budget bums."

We broke out laughing. **My girls are my ride or die babies...** To say my girls came into this world wanted would be a lie. My girls and I went to the AB clinic to take the baby out. At the time I thought it was one. But as I got off the elevator my whole world stopped. I started shakin, feeling real dizzy, almost passing out. J held me up while LaLa called the nurse. They rushed me to the back not to scare the other women who came to get the same thing I was. I sat there not knowing what came over me. The nurse came in asking a whole bunch of question.

"Miss Whyte you say you should be about three weeks right?" "Yes."

"Well that can't be. Your urine shows a different picture."

"So what? Can we just get on with the AB?"

"Yes but it will cost more." "No problem I got it."

"I need you to sign some more paper." After signing my life away the shakes came back.

"I need to go to the ladies room."

"Right threw them doors."

As I entered the bathroom this feeling crept up on me. At first I tried to shake it off but it kept coming at me. I went to turn out the bathroom to get away from it when I heard it. I heard Auntie L and mama Betty voice.

"Chyna what you doin in this place?" I looked up and there they where clear as day, Mama and Auntie L. "Chyna. You goin against the fam?"

"No auntie I would never go against the fam."

"Then why are you here?" "Mama it's hard. Having a baby will be harder."

"SO! You've been taught well you can do it and we got your back, plus you've been blessed twice."

"Twice!" "Yes Mama, baby is having twins." "Twins."

With that being said I walked out the clinic with my twins. The twins was born, identical, one weighing 7lbs 11 ounces the other 7lbs 12 ounces. They where beautiful. They had jet black hair, light brown eyez, pretty baby lips. When they handed them to me I knew there names would be Lynda and Betty, after my mother and Auntie. It was the family thing to do. Raising the twins was a full time job. Between working and being a mother my social life came to a halt. That's how this nigga T got me. Being out of the mix for a minute was an understatement. When I met T you can say I was dick hungry. Fuck it I was feein. He was about 5'11, built beautiful. He had a eight pack, dark brown eyez, a ceaser that showed off his waves, plus a smile that belonged on a tooth paste commerical. I was on my way out of my daughter's school when I spotted him he was posted up on my car.

"May I help you?" "Yes you can. I watched you when as you got out your car. Your walk is dangerous."

I knew this was corny, but it's been a long time.

"I was hoping to take you out sometime."

"Really?" "Really. Do you have a cell? Maybe I can call you."

He was boring me, but my pussy was saying something else.

"Here's my cell. Try me later."

And with that I was gone. Damn her body sick, I can't wait to test that. Alright Susie, get back in my panties. We'll get that later. All the way home into my condo my mind was on T. He was built serious smelled good and had a nice grill. It had been a while sense I felt a man's touch or even had the kitty stroked so to say I was in need was an understatement.

"Ma what we eatin tonight?" "I took out steak."

"That sounds good. Can we get fries and salad with that?"

"Sounds good." "Ok call us when dinner ready."

With that I started cooking. Just then my cell phone rang.

"Hello Chyna, this T. Did I catch you at a bad time?"

"No I was cooking for me and the girls." "Can I join ya'll?"

"NO!" "Dam baby don't be that way."

"T please I don't know you like that to have your ass around my girls."

"Enough said. To be honest you where working that business suit today. Do you always dress like that?"

"No but when you run shit at a money getting company you dress the part."

"I see you get it in, and the them twins of your's are beautiful. They look just like their mom." "Thank you." "Do you know what your doin on Friday?"

"Nothing that I know of." "Can you get someone to stay with the twins so you can ride out with me?"

"Is this your cell # that came up on my phone?" "Yeah."

"Let me get back at you about Friday." "One."

I called my girl Lala - Lala loved these girls. You've thought she was their mother.

"Make it do what it do." "Hey girl what's up?"

"Hey Chyna what's the matter?" My goddaughters sick?"

"No they're fine. I need you watch them Friday. I don't want to leave them by themselves." "I got my girls. Hold up bitch where you goin?"

"Well noisy I got a little somen- somen date with this nigga I met over by the girls school."

"His name?" "T." "Do he sell cd and shit?" "Yeah why you know that man?"

"Not personally. I coped some cd and shit from him. C that nigga looks good and he draped in the hot shit." "I know he was rocking Roca Wear from head to toe with them crispy Timbs." That's him. That man stay in that Roca Wear shit."

"I'll see my girls on Friday later ma."

Friday couldn't get here no faster. All I thought about was rolling with T. I was excited. The last time a man touch me he was pulling my twins out my puss and sense becoming a mother hanging out took back seat, not tonight. When the office clock struck 5pm I practically ran out the building.

"Miss Whyte, Mary yelled." "You forgot your papers and purse."

Thanks is all I could say as I headed out to pick up the twins from school and head to Lala house over on the west side. As I pulled up on 135th and Amsterdam I saw Black, KK and Nene my stomach did flip flops, not for Black's sorry ass - it was that nigga KK. KK was still getting it and he was gorgeous. That 6'6 frame, long eyes lashes, skin was silk like smooth dark caramel; he had that well groomed goatee framing his luscious mouth. My girl done there grew wet just looking at him. I stepped out the Range. Nene noticed us first. I was still sporting my business suit as I walked around to help my girls with their bags. All eyez was on us as we made our way across the street. Black started running his mouth.

"How my girls doin?" "You must be talking to someone else cause we're not your girls." "Chyna why you need to stunt on me? I was just checking on my girls."

Before it got ugly in front of my girls Nene spoke.

"Can I take the girls to the store?"

"Go ahead I'll be right here when you get back."

My focus went back to Black. Bitch ass.

"Black I'm not goin show my true colors right now but let me make this crystal clear so you don't get it fucked up the next time you see me and mine."

"Miss us with that how my girls doin." "You don't do a damn thing for my daughters from not visiting them to buying the clothes on their backs or the food in their stomachs." "Stop stuten for your boss's."

KK broke out laughing. Black looked like he wanted to leap, but KK put that on smash. "Don't even think twice about it!" "I break something off nasty in that ass!"

Black and me both looked at KK, amazed. With that being said I took my daughters and bounced.

"Black what's up with that?" "You don't take care of yours."

"It's not that - that bitch Chyna hard body she be ridding with a nigga one minute then ready to dead a nigga the next. I can't get with that. I'm the man in the game not her."

"Holding your seeds down is only right. You don't even do that nigga."

"That's true, but I don't believe their mind." "What you mean nigga?"

"What I mean in my heart of hearts, I don't feel their mind."

"Whatever nigga those yours."

Black felt wounded. Not only had he been played in front of his comrades, but they where on her side. He knew now wasn't the time he would get Chyna back.

"Black we out we'll get up with you later."

KK and Nene hoped in the Mercedes and rolled out.

"KK what was all that back there?"

"You know me better than anybody Nene, I don't play that shit - especially when kids involved."

"I know that I'm not speaking on that I'm talking about what was not said."

"The way your body spoke when Chyna pulled up."

KK knew what his sister was talking about, her spelling it out spoke volumes. KK had a thing for Chyna from the first time he saw her. He was down town in Soho shopping he never liked looking like the typical block nigga. So he only shopped for the best. He had just stepped out of the Phat Parm boutique when he spotted her she was home and she was coming out of Chi-Chi spa. She had this glow about her even though she was big she still walked like she was light as a feature KK love voluptuous women there was nothing a slim chick could do for him or with him. He needed cushion for the pushin and Chyna fitted that bill on more ways than one. 5'2 if that, she had small hands and feet but that's where the smallness stopped. Everything else was steak and potatoes with butter and gravy. She had breast that was begging to be sucked, hammocks for legs, face to die for. Not to leave it out - if you had to ask what stood out all you had to do was watch her walk away. She had an ass a man could get lost in and sleep on at night. What KK love about her most was the way she carried herself. She wasn't one of the around the way girls always in everybody business always in the clubs and no nigga every spoke bad about her. That's because she never shitted where she laid her head and that stood out to KK. Lately he been hooking up with dumb bitches; they pretended to be smart but once he got with them the facade was over and KK was gone.

"KK you listening to me?" "I hear you Nene and you're right I'm digging shorty but you know how I get down." "I'm with Meka and I'm cut loyally from the bone."

"Whatever nigga that's not who you want." "I know but that's who I'm with enough said." "Good. Now that is over, Nene put a nigga on Blacks ass. That man didn't take that situation lightly. The look on his face said he was goin to try to get even." "Done!"

J was sitting at the table in One Fish Two Fish when in walked Black. He was fuming. He had just got clowned in front of his peoples and told to hold his by the man who could kill him with a snap of his finger. Black look over in the corner noticing J.

"What up J?" Nothing what up with you?" "Nothing, who you here with?"

"Nobody. Lala babysitting. Chyna seeing some nigga, I'm solo tonight."

"Cool, then it came to Black, can I join you?" J thought about it- it's been a while sense her girl spoke on Black.

"Why not sit down." Black order a shot of Hennessey and Long Ice tea for J.

"So what do I owe the pleasure?"

"Nothing ma you and me always been cool, it's me and Lala who can't vibe, feel me?"

"I feel you. It's just that Lala loves Chyna. They go way back. If you fuck with Chyna then you fuck with Lala." "And you?"

"I do me but don't get it fucked up if my phone rings. I ride with my girls."

They exchanged small talk for a while once the liquor kicked in J loosened up and was feeling herself. J was getting hot. She started remembering the sexcapades Chyna use to tell her about Black. Black could see it in J eyez. She was hot so he went in for the kill.

"J let me take you home." "Ok."

Black paid the bill and they where gone. They reached 1199 J was horny as hell and with her man Roc in prison she was in need of some dick.

"You coming up for a night cap?" "I got Hypnotic and Belve."

Black hoped out and followed J upstairs. He never noticed how good J looked until tonight. J had on Apple Bottom jeans that look painted on her cherry shape ass, a wife beater with some fresh Uptowns her hair was pulled up in a ponytail with one dread hanging out the back. They rode the elevator in silence. Once they entered her place it was all over. J closed and locked the door once she turned Black backed her up against the door stuck his tongue in her mouth J opened wide. She hadn't felt this good in a while. They kissed like they'd been fuckin for minute. Black ran his hands all over her body, stopping at her breast he squeezed and pinch them, threw her wife beater. This shit had J remesencing about the first time her and Roc fucked. J moaned, creaming her panties. She pushed him back, wanting him to see her expose her goodies. Black's mouth fell open with her clothes on she was something but with her clothes off she was bad. Black stayed focused on J's body while undressing, never loosing eye sight of J. Now it was J turn to stare. She couldn't believe it; her girl wasn't lying when she said this nigga was holding 9 ½ inches of dick. J lead Black to the living room she turned on the cd player. Jill Scott was rockin. J turned on the AC and bent on her knees she crawled over to him. Black opened his legs wider so she could get a good spot to suck him off. J started with his balls licking and tea bagging them one by one then both at the same time. This shit turned Black on. He lit his blunt and relaxed. J was eating and sucking Black's dick. J was dick hungry. Roc had been gone a minute she wanted to taste all of him she spit on the tip running her tongue all between the slit. Black was goin crazy. "Put it in your mouth."

J did as she was told. She sucked and deep throat Black's dick for what seem like forever.

Black was in lala land. His blunt was easing his mind while J was blowing his back out with the monster head. Just when he thought it couldn't get no better she started humming with the song sucking him off to the beats of Jill Scott. He was so hard he started to cum. J was ready to taste that sperm all in her throat. He pumped her mouth two more time and let loose all down her throat. J took it like champ once she got ever bit down her throat J eased up and straddled herself across Black's lap. He guided the head to the hole of her pussy and shoved her down on it. J shrieked from the pain, never once trying to get off it. About a couple of strokes in it J was riding that dick like a champ.

"J your pussy wet." "I know this dick got me cumming like crazy."

That's when Black the beast showed up. He pulled out, threw J ass over the arm of the couch and rammed his dick in her little cherry ass. J hollered from the pain.

"Black what you doin that shit hurt?" "Shut the fuck up and take it. You wanted the dick, right?"

Black grabbed J by the waste and tore her a new asshole. J tried to stop him but he had her he was all up in her ass.

"So you like fuckin your girl baby daddy? You like this dick? Tell me you like it."

J's dumb ass thought if she kept quite he would stop. That shit just drove him crazy.

"Say you like it whore, say it." "I like it, I like it." 'So you do."

Black was a straight caught up in this revenge J was goin to pay for Chyna's mistake. Black drove his dick into her ass a couple more times then pulled out. He grab the back of her, hair pulling her face into his balls.

"Smell me bitch, that's your ass all on my dick." Now open that pussy up."

J laid back on the couch while he fucked her pussy walls swollen. Black saw the fear on J's face. He had done what he came to do, to drive it home. He bent down whispering in her ear.

"Tell your girl Chyna next time she bark on me in front of my peoples this will happen to the twins." I don't give a fuck about her or those bitches!"

Black pulled out and cam all over her face, leaving J on the couch torn and swollen. J was stuck. What had she done" In the back of her mind she wanted to do it, to hurt Chyna like Chyna did her man. This was just the big pay back to Chyna. J knew that Black would tell Chyna and when she ask J why she would remind her about Roc, but the plan went all wrong. Black was the one who got revenge. Another win for Chyna. **That Bitch....**

Chapter Five

Lesson Five: Everybody Who Smiles Up in Your Face isn t Always Your Friend..

As Black walked out the door the phone rang. J was hurtin bad. She could barely move. She knew who was calling; he called everyday at this time. J made her way to the phone. She hurt bad, not only her body but emotionally. She had fucked her girls' baby father and cheated on Roc. J picked up the receiver.

"Collect call from Attica, press one to accept two for no." Once J hit one Roc started in. "What's up baby what took you so long to answer the phone?"

"I was sleeping boo," J just lied. "You know a nigga call this time everyday"

"I hear you what's up?" "Nothing much I just miss my baby."

"I miss you too." "I wish you where here so I could suck on that good dick."

"In due time baby, in due time - now onto business."

"Is everything goin alright out there?" "There you go is that all you think about? Getting back at that girl? Can't we talk about us for once? Dam Roc."

Roc was heated. J knew the plan from the word go. Now she was acting like she wanted out or to be that bitch real friend. He couldn't spit venom over the phone knowing it was tapped so he switched gears.

"Baby you right, let's talk about us. I got 32 days left then I'm all yours, big dick included." J was back on track. Roc was her man and she do anything for him and vice versa. They continued to talk for another five minutes about nothing special.

"You have 1 minute left." "Roc baby I'm with you 100%. It's me and you against the world."

"That's my boo stay on that target. Love U."

J ran herself a bath with Carol Daughter chocolate bath balls. Her whole body ached. She had only plan on fuckin Black then dismissing his ass. That planned back fired big time. Her shit got twisted something bad. Chyna was the one to blame. If she hadn't bark on the nigga she wouldn't be in this situation. This just added to the shit she started to hate about her so- called friend. Chyna was becoming a problem. First she held the top shit. Condo on the top floor, she drove all the top shit Range, Mercedes and BMW. Two beautiful girls who stayed flyer then her. When she spoke about getting a job at American Express the bitch got it, not knowing J applied for the same position. They turned her down.

J's plan with Roc was sealing itself more and more. She just needed to keep playing her role until her man was home to execute the plan. With that J eased back into the tub to let the hot water take affect. Black didn't know it, but his every move was being recorded and told to KK by his right hand man Steve. Steve put a call into Nene.

"What up my dude?"

"Nothing thought you like to know that man Black just left old girl best friend house." "Who Lala? No the other chick." "Good lookin. Keep on that kid."

"With what you paying me, I should be that nigga draws."

Laughter broke out among gangsta.

"KK guess what? Steve just put in my ear our boy Black hitten Chyna best friend J." "Stop stuntin." "No Steve on him good, put someone on her to her man Roc. He owes big time. I need to see that man when he step out."

"Let me make a call to our girl Lady."

"Hello ladies, how god mommies girls doin?" "Well hello to you to bitch."

"Oh someone jealous. "God mommies baby hear that? Mother sound jealous."

"God mommy you two crazy." "No baby she a bag of crazy by herself."

"Then your nuts cause you hang with me." "True!"

"We stop at the store, but now looking at all this shit here there was no need. What's all this?" "Their goin to stay the weekend. So you can get your oil change."

"There is a God, because mother needs it."

"Good now be gone so I get the latest gossip on school and shit."

"Say no more girl's mother is leaving the building." "Love you always." "Love you too." Baby and Lil Mama hollered. Riding back to my house my body danced just thinking about T. He was getting it tonight if he played his hand right. Once inside my house I poured me a glass of Apple Bacardi mixed it with apple Snapple over crushed ice. Stired it with my finger, then sipped long and slow, letting the coldness take affect on my dry mouth. I picked up my remote hit selection 3 Floetry. Lit my Bath and Body Works vanilla scented oil came up out my work clothes laid back on my Channel suede armor chair. Letting the oil take over my body it had been a while since I had the condo all to myself. It felt good after basicing in the scent along with Floetry. I started my jet stream deep bath tub adding vanilla bath beads with bubbles. My candles flickered around the tub. Down went my lights as my feet melted into the water. My cell phone rang.

"Make it do what it do." "Chyna this T, wanted to confirm 9." "9 it is."

With that I lost myself in my silky bath. While my body soaked all my mind could do was think about KK. That man could get it any which way he wanted. The more I thought about him the more my body wanted to feel his touch while laying back. Letting the jets do their thing I allowed my mind and body to go there. KK was standing in front of me with only his timbs on. He had this look in his eyez like he was goin to hurt something. That something lie between my legs. He started with kissing my forehead then my eyez. My body shivered with his touch. He traced my lips with his warm tongue then he opened my mouth and slid his tongue in and out, making sucking sounds. He had me. He turned me over on my stomach, pulling my ass up in the air. Diligently he began placing kisses on it, first pecks then long kisses. With his thumb he penetrated my ass; this made my asshole soaking wet. KK slid his tongue down the middle of my cheeks landing in the land of Susie Q. He slurped until Susie Q poked all the way out.

"That's it KK, eat Susie Q. She like your tongue."

My man KK was on a mission he wanted Susie to talk so he went at her like a dog chasing a bone, biting licking and sucking so hard.

"I yelled out. Please don't stop."

"Is that Susie talking or you Chyna?" "No it's her. Then let her speak."

Back at my pussy KK went. I tossed in the tub not wanting this fantasy to stop.

"KK this is Susie Q speaking. Tongue fuck me. I want to cum. KK I'm about to gush." "Do it for me."

I climaxed harder than ever. Woo- woo, I opened my eyez in the tub sweating and breathing hard I washed my body and climbed out. My outfit for tonight was my DKNY black rap around dress with my DKNY sandals, gold clutch and underneath was my Hips and Curves all in one thong piece. I finished it off with Donna Karen Cashmere perfume threw on my Mac lip gloss and headed out the door. I climb into my car my phone went off. MJB singing. When that came on I knew who it was.

"Make it do what it do." "Chyna I need to holla at you it's important."

"Can it wait until tomorrow? I'm on my way out."

"No problem but get with me soon it's very important."

"No doubt J first thing tomorrow." While driving my mind wondered what did she get herself into now? Please lord not tonight. I need this. I noticed a parked car in front of Mannies, the black Range Rover. KK Range, his stood out. He let Flex kill it. Nobody had KK's custom made shit and he knew it. That shit stood out just the way he liked all his shit. Only thing was my butter cream Range kilt his every time I pulled up where his was. I strolled into the restaurant and sure enough there was Meka and KK.

T spotted me. As I made my way to the table I decided to stop and speak to the love birds.

"What's good Meka hey KK how ya'll doin?"

Meka grab KK's hand. "We doin it Chyna."

KK didn't seem to share that thought. He went for it though, not to embarrass her.

"Ok I got to go. Someone waiting."

KK looked at T then back at me.

"Be careful Chyna. I seen that man in action." "Thanks for the heads up. Enjoy."

As I walked away I couldn't help but feel eyez all over me. Sure enough as I peaked back KK was staring through my dress. I liked it. I liked it so much my ass almost tripped. Meka noticed KK watching too. "Are you done?" KK turned his attention back to Meka. "Watch your tone when you talk to me and miss me with that bullshit. Our shit ain't rockin like you stated to Chyna,"

"So you want Chyna now!" (eyez rolling)

"No I just don't like liars and you just lied so what else you been lieing about?"

Meka knew she fucked up with that move. She been creeping on the low with one of KK's workers and the shit was starting to get to her. Meka was a dumb bitch - she knew how to bring a man in but she couldn't keep him for nothing, so when KK stepped to her she thought she had it made. But keeping KK took more than the bomb ass head and dick ridin - a chick had to have a brain, a goal and know how to cook. A Queen like his mother, was to his father. Neither of these Meka had. All she posed was a mean sex game. Meka worked at American Express also, but she was a bottom bitch. She didn't play with the big boy's like Chyna did. She worked in the mailroom. Meka was a low budget chick always acting like she had but never did that's until she came up on a scam. She was stealing social security numbers off dead people and applying for credit cards under their names. She had her system on lock. She would feel out the application and submit them, then have them sent to different PO Box's. How I came upon the 411? I had eyez every where. Like my nigga Biggie said, I got lawyers watchin lawyers. Meka went from Steve Madden to Jimmy Choo; it just didn't make sense. Mailroom paid alright but even with over time she couldn't shop on 5th with us Boss Bitches. I sent my #1 eyez in my brother from another mother Mike. We came up together on my Auntie L's block. Mike's mother was a crack head to the third power. Mike came to us after his mother tried to sell him to Auntie L for a hit. We knew we had to keep him before he end up dead or somebody's boy toy. Mike was always getting into trouble, robbing, stealing or puttin a beating on somebody. He was still my brother 4 life. He was on parole when I got the word.

"Sis I need a favor." 'What for this time?" (faced twisted)

"It's not like that. I need a job or they're throwing my ass back to the wolfs."

"Say no more. Be down by my job; I'll put you to work." "Good looking sis."

From there I put him to work in maintence picking up people shit and letting me know who and what was trying to take my position and who was doin who and what. I needed to know how Meka was maken her extra money. I knew if anyone would know or find out for me my brother would. I came stepping off the elevator in the basement.

"Hey Jeff you seen Mike?" "Yeah he in back getting dressed. So Boss lady when can I taste that?"

"Never nigga, now lay off my baby sister before they find your ass in the furnace."

"Mike please I was just joking." "Brother, let me holla at you for a minute."

"What's up baby sis?" "That chick Meka in the mailroom. What you got on her?"

"A whole lot." "Let's pick this up after work at BBQ's on 73rd n 3rd on me."

While going about the rest of my day mad shit ran through my mind. What did Mike have on her and was he involved. I love my brother but givin up my corner office and six figures was not something I was gonna do. BBQ's was jumping as always - nice music nice crowd. My brother had beat me there.

"Patron, good nigga? Couldn't wait on a chick?"

"That's my sis back in the hood." "Ya feel me?"

"Your brother ordered you a Apple Martini." "Spill it my dude."

"What you need to know?" "Everything… From how she got on to her hook up."

"Well old girl Meka is definitely scheming. She running a credit card scam big time." "How you know this and first are you in on it." "Never! I wouldn't bring the heat to your spot." "You know I love you to much for that." "Back to Meka. How I caught on - one night I was cleaning the back of the mailroom and when I came out she was there writing numbers off people's application, but only the returned ones for the deceased."

"That shit seem out of place so I kept watchen her ass always on the 1st and the 15th when the new cards came in she was in there deep." "I stepped to her one night. She almost shit herself." "What you still doin here?" "My job, and you?" "Nothing. Goodnight Mike, she said, then she jetted." "On her way out she dropped one of the application." "Me being on my job I picked it up put it in my pocket waiting to give it back to her." "That night curiosity got to me. I peeked at the paper and there it was, another woman name, PO address, everything she needed to complete the application." "Me being the business man I checked it out and found out the chick was dead but Meka was using her government and the deal is working."

"How, you know?" "After comin up on her scam I started showing her mad attention, brushing my dick up against that fat ass, then one night while we alone in the basement I lick that pussy clean giving her the 9 all in that ass - she likes that."

"TMI nigga. I didn't need to know that part."

"You asked so let a nigga finish. "So after that night in the basement we started hanging tuff. One night she invited me over. When a nigga reached her projects I was shocked; her apartment was straight out of a dam magazine." "She had wall to wall carpet throughout except for the bathroom and kitchen - they had slated tile. Her living room was sick, painted burnt orange with Neman Marcus sectional all in creamy gold with the table and lamp set to match." "The table look like blocks - it had holes in it for wine and shit. She had a 42 inch, all that boss shit." "She cake up like that?" "That's what a nigga though to. But after puttin that ass to sleep with this good dick." "Here we go, I told you that part is TMI." "Anyway, I peeped the cards on the coffee table. I counted them she had like fifteen with I.D. to match - whoever does her ID's knows their shit. Them shit look like the real thing." "Let me get this. She has no money but her card game is wicked." "Yes, they're long because she took your boy shopping and charged over 5 thou that day alone. When your big brother was done my apartment looked like hers." "I hope you didn't have that shit sent to your real address or back to the wolfs you go and." "She did it as a present and it was delivered to a bogus address her girl gave her so I'm clean ,and I left that ass alone. She to dam insecure for me once you get with her she constantly calling a nigga, wantin you by her side. She not that bright, she can't keep up in a conversation and her ass can't cook. You would think she can burn with her ass being all big and pretty. All she know how to do is order out and she orders from every joint around her way."

"Mike you my brother, but you ain't about shit." "You get your gear, apartment funky then gone like the wind." "You know how I do. I love em and leav em alone. (smiling)

That's my brother the whore…(laughing)

Chapter Six

Lesson Six: Learn to Listen to Your Gut÷.

T stood as I made my way over to the table. His mind goin a mile a minute and his toy was growing harder as I moved closer.

"Hello Chyna." "Hello to you to."

"You look good enough to eat." "Thank you. You look handsome, smelling all good." "You know my man KK?"

"Yeah he good people, why?"

"I noticed ya'll talking. "Oh, so you watching me?" "No, well maybe."

"He was just giving me some good advice that's all."

"Ok let's get back to you - you know I eyed you from the time your feet hit the pavement out of your car all the way to the school." "So you do watch me?" (smiling)

"Ma I'm just saying you got it in all the right places and more." "He smirks."

"Thanks again T. Not to be rude but, my name is Chyna and are we goin to talk about my body all night?"

"Sorry it's been a while sense I seen a big girl work it like you. You have a sway to your walk and you dress to your size, not like them other women wearing shit just because they made it in their size."

"Sure you're right that shit always kill me when I see my big queens in clothes they have no business wearing."

"Let's order and see where the evening leads."

Sipping on my drink I wonder about KK. He looked so good sittin over there.

"A penny for your thoughts." He says.

"I'm sorry just thinking."

"I hope it's about us."

"T, there's no us. We just met."

"Well let me cut all the bullshit and place my cards on the table."

"Let them hit then."

"No doubt I want you Chyna. I wanted you for a minute."

"That's it, you want to fuck me? Why did't you state that from the gate?"

"Chyna you a boss chick so I didn't know how to come at you. Now that I got you here let's do it."

"You know what T, let's do the damn thing. Susie need a good licking."

T paid for our drinks and we left. We made our way to the Holiday Inn in Soho. Once in the room we made small talk while I made sure I had my condoms.

"Let me freshen up a lil bit then it's go time." "No problem."

I went into the bathroom, pulled out my Summer's Eve wipes, wipe the kitty and sprayed my Cashmere all over then headed back into the room. While in the bathroom T had a trick of his own. He wanted me totally under his spell so he tap my drink with X just to get me extra loose. This should get that body goin. Ms. Chyna don't know what I have in store for her ass. I step out the bathroom with nothing on but my thong and sandals, ready for a good licking.

T almost drop his drink. When he turned around he licked his lips, handed me my drink.

I swallowed with one gulp. This made him happy, a little to happy for me I shoved it off. T laid me down on the bed and went to kiss me. I stopped that quick.

"We here to fuck not fall in love, right?" "Right."

He moved on, his tongue traced down the middle of my breast, making circular motion. This was making me horny. He put my left breast in his mouth, licking the areole, then switched to the right breast. He was teasing me. My body was hot, too dam hot. He wasn't eatin my pussy. T parted my legs, fingering my clit, makin me wet. In went one finger, then two. Before I knew it he had four fingers in me. The feeling was good but I couldn't fuckin move. I wanted to. My body was stuck no words would come out, neither. Then there was another person on me. I heard voices but couldn't see anything. My eyelids were real heavy and my head wouldn't move.

"Hey T she a pretty thing."

It was a female voice. It was another female in the room. My ass was cooked. T did spiked my drink. Now there she was on me.

Fuck! KK's words came back to me. Be careful, I heard about that man…

"I know she pretty and her pussy real wet." "Then let's do it."

She climb on the bed and started suckin my tits. Trying to put hers in my mouth.

I couldn't move to stop her. T was between my legs tearing at my pussy with his mouth.

I was scared there I was rendered motionless, couldn't defend myself as the two took turns at my pussy. **I cried.** All I could hear was KK telling me to be careful then T stuck his dick up in me and proceeded to fuck the shit out of me.

"This some mean pussy. Shit hot and tight."

"Let me taste it." "Don't worry there's enough here for you ma."

T fucked me in every position he could think of then he let his girl have at me. She ate me out while T fucked her.

"Eat the pussy baby she got some sweet juice coming out. Taste it baby, aint that shit sweet?"

"Yea baby. look she getting ready to squirt."

"Let me get that." "No I want it, you had yours."

She got up and put her pussy on my pussy and girl fucked me. After making me cum for the umpteenth time T decided he had enough of me and the show.

"Let's boogie, she will come to soon and we don't need to be here."

They left me there butt naked and fucked out my mind when I finally woke up the maid was knocking on the door.

"Clean up time, do you want your room clean?"

"No thank you, I yelled, falling off the bed."

My stomach felt like I'd been kicked by a hoarse. I could barely stand. I crawled into the bathroom, turned on the shower and sat my entire body under it.

Sitting there I tried to remember what happened. One thing I do remember: I was violated and that **T NIGGA WAS A DEAD MAN WALKING..** I cleaned myself up, made my way out of the hotel, noticing the front desk person who checked us in last night.

"Hello Peter, is that right?" "Yes,"

"Can I talk to you for a minute in private?"

Once we where alone I pulled two crispy 1000 dollar bills. I had Peter's total attention. "Did you notice anyone or did anyone ask for me and my friend room?"

"Yes she didn't give a name she was light skinned, about 5'6, dark brown hair. She had hazel eyez."

"Thank you, here's a tip for your services." Now I knew who help T violate me.

SHAYA WAS A DEAD BITCH WALKING TOO.. First thing first, I need to hit my girls up. Time to put in some work. I hollered at Lala first.

"Make it do what it do."

"Lala take the twins to their friend Monique's house, I need you."

"Chyna what's the matter?" "Not over the phone, we need to do this in person."

"I'll call J and you can meet us back here." "ONE."

Chapter Seven

Lesson Seven: Don t Get Caught Sleepin On the Next Bitch!

Shaya and T made there way back uptown, both thinking about what just took place.

"T you think that bitch Chyna goin to remember anything?"

"No, I put enough of that X in her to keep her memory foggy. But why you pick her?" "Cause that slut bucket always gets what she want and she got something I really wanted."

"What might that be?" "Blacks baby!"

"So this shit is over a piece of dick? Are you kidding me? You had me play her body like a drum because she took a piece of dick from you!"

"No motherfucker. Not just any piece - my dead baby father. Black was sleepin with me before he ran into Ms. Chyna and skated on me for her".

"I remember the night he broke out I had just told him I missed my period and he was goin to be a father. That man laughed all up in my face then said, well do what you must do, but I'm out." "I hooked this boss chick now it's my turn to come up so I'm gone." "My fuckin blood starting boiling. Before he knew it I was all over his ass, kicking and swinging. We went at it for about ten minutes, then he sucker punched my ass in the chest and stuck his Timbs in my stomach. That shit had me hollering out in pain. He could care less though he stepped over me and left. I lost my baby that night, all for a boss bitch name Chyna. Once I recouped it was on with the bitch. I knew I couldn't go straight at her- her and her team mean with the hands and guns so I needed to come at her another way. When Black kicked her to the curb her ass was fair game."

"So we sexed her to get back at her. What kind of bullshit is that Shaya?"

"No my man I taped the whole shit to show Black that bitch aint about nada."

"You sure you want to do that? He got shorties with that brood."

"From what I hear he don't even acknowledge them. This here tape will get me my man back - another chance to having his baby, the one he really wants."

"If you say so. You better hope it don't back fire on your ass. Holla at your boy if you need another chick dug out or Chyna again - her pussy sick."

Shaya thought about what T had just spit. Could this back fire on her? Just then she thought of another way to come at Black. While driving Shaya dialed Black.

"Who dis?" "Black it Shaya. I need to see you, where you at?"

"I'm with my peoples right now. What you want?"

"I have something I need you to peak at."

"Alright come through 155 Fredrick Douglas Blvd building 22 apt 1."

"Black who the fuck you got coming through here."

"Nene she just one of my jump off." "What she want?"

"Don't know, she said I'll see when she get here." "She better not bring no bullshit."

"If it is she can suck me and KK off and you can watch."

"Nigga who the fuck you talking to? Do I look like some third wheel? I'm a boss chick who only fuck boss bitches, remember that!"

Black sat his ass back on the couch. He knew he fucked his self; but the words had already left his mouth. All he could do was pray, for whatever Shaya had was good enough to take the heat off him. It seemed as if time stood still. On Black's ass where was Shaya he had two killers twins at that he was sweatin. Shaya knocked at apt 1. Black ran for the door. Shaya stepped in. She didn't expect to see KK and Nene. Shaya though about changing her mind. Black looked good so she went with the plain.

"What's good ma?" "Nothing much, just thought you would like to peep something on your baby mother." When KK heard that he was all ears.

"About my babies mom - what the bitch do or buy now?"

"If you have a DVD player I can show you better than I can tell you."

They all gathered around the TV while Black push play. First it look like a porno; a nigga eatin a bitch out while another sucked on her breast. Black took a closer look and recognized the body. Chyna, yes it was her getting her shit twisted. A wicked smile crept across Shaya's face. The more the movie played the closer she thought she was getting her man back and her baby too. KK and Nene watched in silence, not believing what was unfolding on TV. The more KK watched the more he found something strange with Chyna's body language. She wasn't moving or saying anything; the look on her face was gone, like she wasn't even there. Then he noticed the other chick in the DVD was sitting in the room.

"How you get yours hands on this?" Nene asked. Black broke out in a loud roar.

"YES! I finally got that bitch. Bet you she won't bark on a nigga no more. You did good Shaya…" As the words left his mouth KK lifted Shaya off her feet pinning her to the wall by her throat. Black jumped up as he reached to help Shaya. Nene stuck the desert eagle to his head, daring that nigga to move. Black froze, knowing he had a killer on him. Shaya was turning colors as KK held her throat.

"My fam asked you a question. Where the fuck did the DVD come from?"

"TTT gave it to me to show Black. He wanted to make him jealous."

"Go ahead." "He told me that Black had taken his girl a while ago so he wanted to get back at him by setting up his baby mother on video."

"You lying bitch. Chyna wasn't down with that. She look like she on something. She not even woke in some of the shots."

"He did have X pills on him, maybe he used them."

"What you mean maybe? The other chick is you! You made a mistake and showed your tattoo on your ass that say SHA-SHA."

The whole room froze again. Black and Nene never peeped that. They where both caught up for different reason on the what was taken place on the DVD.

"KK please let me go so I can finish. T knows I like chicks too so when he asked would I be down for a threesome I was all in without knowing who the other chick was. When I got there Chyna look like she was all in."

"Cunt you lyin. It's ok because it's not you that I want. Where that nigga T at?"

"Truth be told I don't know. He said something like he was goin away for a while."

"Say no more. Now get gone before I kill you instead."

Shaya and Black walked outside. "What was all that about?"

"Nothing boo, I'll be by tonight. Keep that pussy warm for me."

Shaya perked up when she heard the word boo; now all she had to do was get T out of town. Killers was out for him. She never meant to get T in this deep but it was either her or him. KK snatched the DVD out. He was in killer mode; he wanted blood. T's blood to be exact. T violated his queen and dying was the only way to pay.

"KK you aight?" "No that nigga took advantage of my queen now he must be touched." "You're Queen. KK Chyna not you girl. Meka is."

KK shot Nene a killer stare. Nene didn't back down. She spoke slow.

"Listen I know how you feel about baby girl. After this I see your feelings run deep so what you goin do about Meka."

"A nigga could care less about Meka, dumbass. "The women that holds my heart is CHYNA.."

Chapter Eight

Lesson Eight: Keep Your Friends Close and Your Enemies Closer.

My girl Lala dropped my twins off. "You two got money?"

"Lil Mama, You know mommy keeps us with stacks."

"Good now take this $200 and you know the rules - ask no one for nothing and NLB"(Never Look Back). "We got you."

Lala loved her goddaughters and would lay a nigga or bitch down for fuckin with them.

"J this Lala." "What's up ma?"

"I need you to meet me at my house. Chyna needs us."

J frowned. She really didn't feel like rolling for that bitch Chyna.

"J you heard me?" "Yes I'm goin to pass, I'm not feeling good."

"J get your ass dressed. I'll be there in 10.

Lala was growing tired of J. She been acting up lately. Something about her just didn't sit right with Lala. Her girls had never met her man Roc and when they where alone without Chyna J always seem to be trying to test her loyalty to her girl. Lala knocked at J's door. "What is it La?" "What the fuck you mean? I told you already we need to roll, so why you still in pajamas?"

"Didn't I tell you I wasn't feeling good?"

"J why you walking funny?"

J tried to play Lala. Get her on her team.

"I'm in real pain." "Ok I'll bite, what happened to you?"

"Lala, before I tell you know I was high, drunk I wasn't in my right mind."

"I got it, you was twisted. Next!" "I was in One fish, Two fish drinking when in walked Black." The mentioning of Black's ass made Lala hot. J noticed.

"Keep goin." "Well he sat and we started talking." "About?"

"Let me finish La. We talked about his daughters how he wanted to be in their life but Chyna won't let him."

J knew she was lying but getting Lala on her team would make getting at Chyna just that much easier.

"Let me tell you J that mark straight talkin out his ass. He don't want to be no daddy."

"I found that out the hard way. We got really drunk and he brought me home he said he needed to use the bathroom. I let that nigga in." "Once he was finish he came in the living room sparked up a blunt. Everything was smooth up until the blunt was gone. After that he switched quick. He jumped on me, tearing off my clothes and pawing all over my body. La I tried to stop him but the blunt and liquor had me weak and that nigga strong." "He went at me fucking me every which way but loose, even in my ass, and that's not it. He fucked me so hard he tore the skin in my ass."

J let tears drop for effects. This shit didn't effect Lala. J went in for the kill.

"Lala that man so grimy that he turned me over made me suck him off until he cam all over my face. To drive it home he told me to tell Chyna if she don't stop barkin on him in front of his Comrades, Baby Girl and Lil Mama would be next."

Lala got up off the couch and headed for the door.

"Lala what you goin do? You know Chyna's not goin listen to us about barkin on Black. That leaves the twins out there."

Lala stopped dead in her tracks. "Yo J let me tell you something. What happened to you is your own fault. You should've never broke bread with that bitch ass nigga but he go anywhere near Baby Girl or Lil Mama the shit I'm goin to bring to that man will be real nasty." "Now I'm gone."

Shit didn't go as J planned. That meant Lala had to go too. Lala was twisted. The thought of Black raping her goddaughters was killing her inside. She needed to speak to Chyna fast! Lala picked up her cell, dialing her girl.

"Where ya'll at? I've been sittin in front of your building for over 20 minutes."

"Chyna listen I need to holler at you." "Lala what's wrong? Where my babies?"

"They're fine. They at their friend Monique's house. But it's about them. I'm on my way stay put."

Crazy shit was running through my mind. What was Lala goin to tell me? What did my girls do? Was they in danger? My head was spinning. T and Shaya just date rape me, J needed to talk to me - what next? The waiting was killing me. I seen my girl Lala pull up. The look on her face read **KILLER**. I hopped out the car and started walking behind her until we where in the elevator. We rode in complete silence. Once we entered her loft she was free to tell all.

"Lala sit down you look like you ready to ride on someone and I haven't even told you what happen to me last night."

"Chyna what I'm about to tell you out ways your story by a long shot."

"Alright ma, let me make us a drink then spill it."

I poured us both Belve on ice then took a seat.

"First, your girl J is losing her fuckin mind. She trying to drive a wedge between us. I don't know why. I'm goin to find out."

"Lala you know J, she don't hold a candle to us or our friendship. She reaching, that's all."

"Anyway listen to this then tell me if she just reachin. I get over there to pick her up she not even dressed. I noticing she walkin funny and shit so I ask her what's good. She proceed to tell me her and Black got drunk at One Fish, Two Fish. He drove her home where they got high and Black supposedly rape her. That shit right there she can miss me with because I know J don't do nothing she don't want to do. Apparently you had pissed Black off so he took it out on her ass and I mean her ass."

While I took all of this in my heart went out to J. Black was a bastard but I never thought he would rape one of my girls until Lala hit me in the heart with her next words.

"Then he cam all over her all the while telling her if you don't lay off of him his next victims will be the twins, as in your daughters my goddaughters."

His words push me right over the edge. T and Shaya would have to wait. The whisper twins needed to be woken up and up they would get. All in Black's brains.

"Lala you know what's next right?" "Say no more. My guns are hot and loaded."

"Good anyone get in the way lay them niggas down."

"You don't have to preach to me twice. So what you had to tell me?"

"It's not important anymore. I have one thing on my mind and his name is **BLACK.....**"

Chapter Nine

Lesson Nine: Don t Bite the Hand That Feeds You÷

Meka was sittin home chillin when her phone rang. "Hello?"

"What's up boo?" Nothing much."

"What's the matter, you horny?"

"You dam right. Every time I reach out to KK he either don't answer or he's too dam busy to spend some quality time."

"Meka, your man is a boss. You know how that shit go, but if you want me to stroke that kitty for you just say the word."

Meka was already hot just hearing his voice. She had to play it off so she wouldn't seem too needy. "Only if you want to."

"Meka you know I want that pussy. If you where my girl I'd stay banging that shit." "Then come make it purr daddy."

"I'm on my way, my shift almost over."

Meka hung up ready for her secret lover. She remembered the first time he fucked her. Smoky came by to drop some money off to her. When she opened the door she was half naked, wearing a Diva style black corset with matching lace boy shorts. Her hair was done up in Shirley Temple curls and she smelled like Black Raspberry Vanilla perfume from Bath n Body Works. Smoky was stuck on what was in front of him. He had loved big girls since he could remember. Lookin at Meka bought a beast out of him. She was gorgeous, her breast was standing at attention, her lips glowed from her lip gloss and her legs was watermelon shape; he needed to slice them open. Meka was expecting

49

KK. She had it all planned. He wasn't goin nowhere without feeding her that dick. What she got was an errand boy.

"Smoky what the fuck? Why you here?"

"KK had some last minute business to handle so he sent me over to give you this."

Meka snatched the envelope and slammed the door. Before it could close Smoky stepped in.

"Smoky what the hell?" "I want to make it right, let me help."

Meka thought about throwing Smoky's ass out but he wanted to help and he was lookin good. Smoky was rockin a Sean John red linen short set that hung in all the right places, crisp uptowns, a platinum diamond chain with the pinky ring to match along with the ear ring. He had kissable lips and black eyez that glowed and right now they where roaming all over her body. Just then Jamie Foxx came blasting from the system(Tonight Let's Get Unpredictable).

"Come here Meka, what you doin?"

Smoky pushed Meka up against the sink and ran his hands down her back. Meka felt his dick all up on her stomach. Her pussy was getting wetter by the minute.

"Smoky, you know we shouldn't be doin this." "Then stop me."

Smoky knew he had her. With that he went back to work, running his tongue down the side of her neck then down to the middle of her breast. Meka melted from his touch; she felt on fire. Any thoughts of her putting Smoky out went right out the window. Smoky licked around the outside of her breast. Meka moaned, hmmm. He pulled one out and played with it between his teeth, then the other.

"Let me breast feed you."

Meka put both breast together and let him feed of both of them. This made Smoky grow hard; he was loving the taste he needed more. Smoky stood up; he needed to feel her flesh on his. He removed his shirt while Meka removed her corset. He laid her down on the cheery wood floor. Before he joined her he opened up the frig to retrieve some ice but choose the grapes instead. He put two in his mouth, then feed Meka's mouth. Then he put a mouth full in his mouth and he opened up her legs, squeezing grape juice on her already we panties and licked at it. Meka was loving this shit. KK hadn't touched her in a while.

"Eat it, please don't tease me." "You want me to eat this fat pussy?"

"Yesss." "Not a problem."

Smoky removed her panties and lapped at her chocolate fudge. He stuck one finger in her fudge then another. He was goin to finger fuck her into a frenzy.

"Smoky, don't stop. Put another one in." "Another one?"

"Yes and don't stop until I cum all over your tongue and hand." "Let it loose."

"You got it boo. Right there keep goin. I'ma cum."

"Cum for me, let me see what you got."

Meka rode Smoky's tongue like a prize bull, moving her ass in circles. Then she locked Smoky's head in place while her body shook for about two minutes, then gushed all over his face and down his throat. Meka, breathing all hard, "let me taste you now". Smoky happily feed her the dick. Meka started slow. She wanted it to feel good to Smoky, licking the tip around the head then all the way in. Before Meka knew it she was sucking Smoky dick like she was dick starving.

"Meka, KK don't give you the dick. This head is working a nigga."

Meka was humming and deep throating Smoky. She missed the whole remark. She was killing Smoky's dick, makin him weak.

"I'm not ready to let loose." Smoky grab the dick away.

"Lay down and put that ass up in the air." Meka laid on the floor, feeling the cold against her breasts. She positioned that ass in the air and wiggled it for show. Smoky climb on her ass like a true stallion first in and out up down. Meka threw her ass back.

Smoky liked this watching Meka pussy take all of his dick. This was a weakness of Smoky a big girl who could take a big dick. He started pounding harder.

"Fuck me baby, fuck me with that big dick."

"Yea ma talk that shit. Do KK hit it like this?"

"No you fuckin me right." "Meka bounce that ass for me, make a nigga cum."

Meka went into over drive, pumping that ass back on the dick.

"Smoky you got it, keep goin." "Shit Meka a nigga about to let go."

"Me too. Smoky do it then." "Ma you first."

"No put yours on my back." Smoky let out a loud noise and squirted that nut all on her back. He was sweating, almost dizzy.

"Dam girl that pussy soaking wet." Meka knew she had a new side kick and cheating on KK would be worth it. Steve was coming from a jump off house when he noticed Smoky coming in the building. He jumped back into the staircase not to get seen. He threw his hoodie over his head drew his strings tight, so all you could see was his eyez. As the elevator closed Steve jumped on. At first Smoky thought it was a jack. He showed his gun handle Smoky played the corner. Smoky stepped off, Steve stayed on. Smoky was good, the kid didn't try anything, so he made his way to his boo's apartment. Steve hopped off at the next floor and took the stairs back down. He peeked out the door and watched Smoky knock on Meka's door. At first he thought he was dropping off something; that went out the door when he saw them kiss and feel each other up before closing the door. Steve was loyal to KK; he kept him feed, money in his pockets and a roof over his head. He knew what he had to do next. KK was sittin in the back of his dounut shop, one of his many fronts, when Steve walked in.

"What it do, my dude?" "Nothin much Frank." Frank was one of many henchmen to KK. "Is KK in the back?" "He with Lady, give him a minute." Steve hung back until Lady walked out, and by the way, she was smiling. He knew KK was about to let her loose on a nigga and that nigga was in for a ride straight to hell with gasoline draws on.

"Steve my man, what brings you through? Shouldn't you be watchin that man Black?" "That man laid up with that Shaya chick, he aint movin. Plus I put a lil solider on him while I handle mine."

"Sure you're right so speak." "Let me holla at you in the back"

KK walked in the back with Steve close behind.

"What's wrong?" "KK you know I'm a straight shooter so her goes. That man Smoky fuckin your wife Meka. I was at shorty's house in Taft and spotted that man coming in the building. I played my hoodie so he couldn't see me. We rode the elevator to Meka's floor where he got off and me getting off at the next floor, taking the stairs back down too hers." "When I looked out the door he was knocking. I thought he was dropping something off so I laid back to see what was up and then I seen that man tongue all up in your wife mouth and she was with it too."

"Good lookin my nigga, you did me right. I suspected she was fuckin someone else but one of my own men never crossed my mind. Now you get back to that nigga Black and this for you. 2Gs, that's for being a real nigga."

"Say no more and keep the money. That one was on me. That man need to get it. Just say when." KK smiled. He knew Steve was his man for life but he didn't want him for this one.

"No that's alright I got something for both their ass's." KK was relieved. He didn't know how he was goin to get rid of Meka. Now it wasn't so hard after all, now Smoky would have to die. KK couldn't let this nigga live; that would make him seem weak and that was one thing he was not. And if his enemies or peoples found out Steve lived to talk about it, one of them would try to test his guns and a weak nigga was a mark for every one gunning for his position.

Chapter Ten

Lesson Ten: Never Lie to Your Kids no Matter What..

I picked the twins up and headed home. So much shit ran through my mind that I didn't realize I had starting crying.

"Mommy what's wrong?" Lil Mama asked. "Yea ma speak to us."

I looked over at my babies smiling. This was the first time in a while I just looked at my girls. They looked so much like their farther, their real father, but they were built like me and had my swagger. I ponder for a minute should I tell them the truth; could they handle it, or should I lie not telling them what a bastard their father was or the man they thought was their father?

"Ma do you hear us?" "We asked you why you crying." Baby Girl asked.

"I'll tell you when we get home." The rest of the ride was done with no talking.

"Ok ma we're home. Let us know who or what has got you crying and how we goin to handle it."

"First, we're not goin to handle anything. Lala and me got this one, do you two understand me?"

"Yes, they both said in unison." That should have sent up a red flag but I went with it.

"Now it goes like this. Your sperm donor Black supposedly rape J last night. They were drinking and smoking, one thing lead to another, then Black rape her from what she say." The twins broke out laughing.

They laughed so hard they had to hold on to each other to keep from falling.

"What's so funny?" Baby Girl looked at me. "Do you really think he raped her ma? J has always been jealous of you. We tried to tell you when you asked us why we weren't feeling her."

"What makes you so sure?" "Please ma, she stay trying to grill us about you or when we're with her. All she cares about is what we do when we're home or what you bought or who you sleeping with." Lil Mama said,

"That's not the icing on the cake. She asked me and my sister what would we do if something happen to you or Lala. Would we want to stay with her or our father."

"When the hell did she ask ya'll that?"

"The last time you made us stay at her house while you did overtime at work. That's why when you came to pick us up we where dressed waiting on the terrace."

"I thought that shit was strange but I shook it to the back of my mind. I was so tired from work. That bitch J living like that?"

"Yes. Now finish ma, we know there's more."

"It's what your father said while raping her, he told her if I don't stop barkin on him that you two would be next to get raped."

"WHAT! Are you for real ma? He said me and my sister would be next."

"Is that nigga crazy? He come anywhere near me or my sister I'm gonna straight mark his ass and the same goes for me…" Now these where my twins ready to die for each other and if I died killing Black I would go in peace knowing that my girls had a bond that no one or anything could break.

"You two are cut straight from the cloth ready to dead anyone for coming at ya'll, but that won't be necessary. When it comes to your father I got something in store for his ass. When I finish with him he won't know what hit him."

"Now I need to talk real talk with you two, no games. The shit that's about to go down with your father and me could get nasty if the plan Lala and I came up with don't work. So I need you two to stick together like glue. Where I see one I want to see the other, got me?" "Yes." "And you know them birthday gifts ya'll got? Keep them with you at all times and remember what ever happens NLB, Never Look Back, no matter what!"

"I love you two with all my heart and would die trying to keep you safe. You two know that right." "Yes ma." My girls were crying. They knew firsthand what I meant by that last statement and didn't even want to fantasize what life would be like without their mother.

"Ok go wash up and get ready for bed." "We love you ma." "I love you too."

Baby Girl said, "What we goin to do? We can't lose ma. I would kill someone first before I lose ma."

"That's not goin to happen. You heard her, she and Lala has something for that bastard Black." "So what does that mean?" "That means we stay close to ma and Lala. When they make their move we'll be there to have their backs. If something goes wrong we'll lay that nigga down ourselves."

"I got you sis let's get them presents out and make sure they're fully loaded, ready for war."

"Hold on Baby Girl I think ma is calling Lala. Let's listen in on the phone."

"Lala what's good? I think your right about J she living foul. After this shit with Black is handle we need to see her."

"I told you something aint right with her or her man." "Fuck her. For right now."

"What's the plan for Black ass.?" "Listen and listen good."

Chapter Eleven

Lesson Eleven: Remember to Burn all Bridges to the End or They May Come Back Together.

Roc was laying in his cell just thinking about the day he would get that bitch back. She had caused him his manhood and his status in high school; she had to pay. Roc remembered the day like it was yesterday. He had talk Lala into coming with him to the back of the staircase. He told her all he wanted to do was talk and maybe kiss. Lala was so happy to have a popular boy who looked so good talk to her that she went for it. Roc was the star football player at Julia Richmond; ass was being thrown at him from every direction. He was 6 feet tall with a body of steel. His legs were toned muscle. He had arms that could carry a ton of bricks on each of them. His faced was chiseled all the way around. To top it off he had braids that hung down to his shoulders. He kept the latest styles and design in his head. Roc beat Lala there to make sure no one would come up. He put his combination lock on the door. When Lala came down the other staircase her stomach was in knots; she had never been alone with a boy and now she was alone with the star quarterback.

"Lala come down. I don't bite, at least not on the first date."

Lala blushed. He mentioned a date. It was official, she was on a date with Roc. Roc started out slow.

"Are you ok Lala?" "Yes I'm just nervous."

"Don't be, I got you. I know, a lot of niggas be tryin to get at you with that light brown skin and bubble butt."

Lala laughed. She like that he noticed her skin and bubble. Lala had it, but didn't know how to work it. She had long brown hair, naturally long, pretty eye lashes, thick in the waste with a bubble ass to complete the package. Roc leaned over whispering in her ear.

"Can I kiss you?" She turned, closed her eyez. Roc licked her lips and stuck his tongue between hers waiting for hers. Lala jumped back.

She didn't know he was goin to us his tongue. She liked it so she grab the back of his head and went in for the kill. Roc wasn't enjoying it; he just played along. That ass was worth it and he was goin to get it. He stuck his hands under her shirt, playing with her little tits. He heard a low moan. Lala was feeling good. The shit was making her hot. She had never felt heat like that between her legs. Roc felt Lala relax so he moved down to her skirt. He slid his hand up her thigh, waiting for Lala to stop him. When she didn't he went in he ran his finger over her panties. They where moist. Roc had her wet. Lala opened her legs a little wider so he could get more room to play with her. Roc zoomed in; he moved her panties to the side, massaging her clit. He tried sticking one finger in but she jumped so he went back to playing with her clit. Lala bit down on his earlobe, squeezing on his toy. Roc toy was hard and ready.

"Lala you ever suck a dick before?" 'No." "You want me to teach you?"

She couldn't say no now. She agreed. Roc took out his dick.

"Lala looked at it like, what's that?" Roc's dick was the size of a donkey's it was 9 1/2 inches long and thick alway to the base and balls the size of oranges.

"Do I have to suck all that today?" Roc laughed at her.

"That was funny. Let's start you off slow, just stick your tongue out and lick it first."

Lala did what she was told. Lala licked it, starting at the head then down the side then back up to the tip.

"Stick it in your mouth." She opened and took it in slow, wrapping her mouth around it, letting it slide on her tongue. It tasted salty but she kept goin, seeing the way Roc closed his eyez and licked his lips she could tell he was licking it. She kept goin.

"You got it ma, keep doing that right there, hold the dick, push it in and out, keeping it wet, deeper La take this dick."

Roc was so caught up in getting his dick sucked he never noticed Lala was almost choking on the dick. When she started gagging he pulled out.

"Dam Lala you had it, why you stop?"

"It was to deep, I couldn't breath." Roc was pissed but he couldn't show it.

"It's ok La, you'll get the hang of it."

Lala felt better. She didn't want Roc telling people she couldn't handle hers.

"So you goin let me hit that?" Lala hesitated for a moment. She wanted to be with Roc but not sexually. Roc noticed her thinking so he moved between her legs, licking at her pussy. Lala was caught off guard but she was feeling it. He licked her outer lips then inside. She opened wider. Roc flickered the clit with his tongue, sucking and blowing on it. Lala was open. She was bouncing on his face, back and forth. She held onto his head, fucking his face.

"I like the way you tongue kiss my pussy. Kiss it again."

"Is it mine? Is this pussy mine?" "Yes Roc it's yours."

"I can hit it right?" "Yes Roc anyway you want it."

Bingo, just what he wanted to hear. Roc sucked on her pussy some more then came up, spreading her legs wider and put his dick up in her tight shit. Lala screamed, that shit hurt like hell.

"Lala, kill that noise before someone comes."

Roc drove that dick inside Lala, shoving it to the back, pounding her walls then pulling half way out then all the way up in her.

Lala shit was wet and gushy. Lala pussy was turning Roc on. Lala was getting use to it. She started loosing up and pumping back. She held onto Roc's ass, pounding her pussy all up on his dick. They where fucking hard, sweat started falling off Roc down on Lala's chest. Lala was squeezing on her titties. This was feeling good.

"Go Roc, run that play on this pussy." They was so into it they never noticed Chyna. That bitch watched for a few and was about to be out of there. If I had just waited she would have been all the way gone. Too late, she heard Lala scream.

"You know you want this. Just be easy and it wont hurt."

"No Roc please stop I don't want this."

"Didn't you say it was mine? Didn't you give this ass to me? So I'm taken what's mine and this bubble ass is mine."

That's when the cunt crept up behind me and kicked the fuck out of me. I fell onto Lala, almost bending my dick in half, then the dumb bitch did it again, this time landing on my nuts. Lighting volts went through my body. I stop breathing and seeing for about 20 seconds. When I opened my eyez Chyna had Lala and they where running up the stairs.

I jumped up, pulled myself together and made my way out the back, and headed home. When I returned to school the following week I had my story all mapped out and ready for the staff but they didn't want me. Cherry Joe and his crew was waiting on my ass.

I entered the locker room lookin for my boys. "Roc, I heard a voice as I turned. Joe was standing in front of me." "What's up Joe?"

"Nothing nigga. My cousin told me about that stunt you pulled on the staircase."

"Joe you know how it goes, they say yes then when you start they cry no. No matter what your cuz said it didn't go down like she thought it did."

"You calling my fam a liar?" "No I'm just sayin it's two side to every story."

"Well the only side I care about is my fam. Roc, here's how it's goin to go down. I can kill your punk ass right here or you can put this flower between your ass and walk the lunchroom line. Take your pick."

Joe showed his gun. I choose option B. I knew Joe would kill me but I figured the lunchroom would be empty since it was hot outside, so walking the line wouldn't be so bad. Wrong. The lunchroom was full. Everybody was in the bitch. Joe told everyone and then some when I entered the lunchroom with my dick swinging and a flower in my ass. They all laughed. I was done. I transferred, leaving that one behind. **But one thing was for sure, that bitch Chyna was goin to pay one day!**

Chapter Twelve

Lesson Twelve: Remember What Goes Around Comes Around÷..

Black and Shaya had been laid up for the past two weeks. They were fucking, playing house.

"Shaya sit down, let me talk to you right quick."

"What's up daddy, you need me?"

"Shaya that trick you and T pulled on Chyna, who really set it up? And don't lie or I'm out."

"I did Daddy. I thought and put the whole plan in motion. I knew Chyna wasn't seeing no one and my boy T know how to get at the ladies so I set him out to get her." "Why?"

"She took everything I loved. She stole you from me and caused me my baby. That bitch had to pay."

"You know that man KK goin to kill T."

"Yea what's up with that? I thought he was fuckin Meka over in Taft projects."

"He is but I think that man got a thing for Chyna on the low and if you want to live you should tell that man where T at or get T the fuck out of dodge."

"Daddy I tried, he's not answering his phone. Every time I call it goes straight to voicemail. If I know that man he laid up with some pussy."

"Just make sure you stay clear of that man because he's gonna die and whoever with him gonna catch it too."

"Look at you Black, all worried about your boo."

"Bitch I'm not worried about your conniving ass. I just don't want KK and Nene looking at me for this."

"Black why the fuck you talk so ugly to me? I showed you that bitch aint shit and how much you mean to me. We've been fucking and hanging for the past two weeks. How much more do you need to see to know I love you."

"Miss me with that Shaya all we doin is fuckin. I'm not trying to wife you or fall in love. You know who my wife is so don't get it twisted. I just hit you off with some thank you dick." "Get the fuck out you bastard and don't come back. I hate your black ass."

"You know what Shaya, grow the fuck up and stop all the acting."

"Black you know what? What goes around comes around and when your shit catches you I hope I'm there to see it."

Shaya didn't know Black's shit had caught up to him and he was about to get it.

"Fuck you Shaya. That's why Chyna pussy is the shit. I seen you muchin on it in the video. That pussy was good wasn't it?"

Black laughed as he walked out. Shaya was on fire. She had let her guard down searching for love from Black and in return all she got was played, laughed at, and to make matters worse that bitch Chyna had won for the third time.

She had two niggas in love with her ass and wasn't even trying. She had to be done off. Shaya didn't know how but she damn sure was going to try. Black walked out the building heading to his truck when he spotted Lala. She was headed his way.

"What's up Black? I need to talk to you for a minute about about J."

Black put his hand on his waist.

"Yo Black it's not even like that. I believe that bitch got what she deserved."

"So what you want?" "Can we talk in your truck?"

Black looked at Lala funny and thought for second.

"Yea why not ma? Let me check you first." He patted Lala down - nothing then hit the switch unlocking the doors on the truck. Steve was watching all this shit go down when he noticed me sliding in the back seat of Black truck.

"Ok let's get in so you can speak your peace."

Lala hoped in first then Black. "So what you want to ask me?"

"All I need to know is did you tell J if Chyan don't stop barkin at you that the twins would be next?"

"No, slut I told her you would be." And stuck the desert eagle to Lala head.

"Smack." Lala kissed the gun. "Nigga please, that shit there don't scare me. But this will." I sat up and stuck the whisper twins to his head.

"Now drive nigga or you can die right here in front of your bitch's house."

Lala snatched the desert eagle, smiling.

"Now do what my girl says and move this bitch." Where?"

"Take us to 120th between FDR and Palendo." "Chyna that's where the abandon steal warehouse at." "EXACTLY. Now drive."

Black started the truck, thinking about what Shaya just hollered at him. If only he could get to KK he would put a stop to both these bitches. He was at a lost; there where three guns on him with two killers behind them. Steve watched not believing the turns of events. Black was caught.

"Nene, you with KK?" "Yes why?"

"Ya'll wont believe this. Chyna and her girl Lala have Black hemmed up in his truck driving somewhere."

"Steve keep following them and hit us when they stop. You got it, loud and clear."

I didn't know it but I had three people following and watching out for me.

When Black pulled up it was pitch dark; the warehouse was abandon except for the cars whizzing by on the FDR. I hoped out first.

"Lala keep that desert eagle on his lame ass." I yanked the door open and grab that nigga by his dick, just thinking I use to suck and ride this shit.

"Get your punk ass out. Funny I don't here you talking now. What that bitch Shaya got your tongue?" Psst, he spit in my face.

"Fuck you and your kids." My girl Lala smack the nigga with the gun, opening up his head.

"Get the fuck in there." When we reached the back there was a chair waiting.

"Sit the fuck down bastard. So you like spittin? I guess this wont bother you."

I tied his ass to the chair, kicked the chair on the floor, pulled my pants down and pissed in his face. He tried not opening his mouth that failed.

"Swallow bitch, Lala laughed." "Get that nigga ma, you go next La."

Lala pulled her pants down and pissed. It was my turn now to laugh. It did look funny, piss raining down on him.

"You can tell the devil you had a golden shower." Then we got down to business. Me and Lala pistol wipped his ass.

"So you goin to rape my babies?" "Fuck them, they where never mine. I told you before don't know baby hold a nigga. And two wasn't goin stop nothing. They don't even look like me."

"So because they don't look like you there not yours?"

"Whatever ma, like I said they aint mine and if I get out of this shit alive what I did to J will seem like child's play compared to what I'm goin to do to Lil Mama and Baby Girl." That shit sent me into a mother's rage, but before I could let loose I heard noise. I turned my guns on who was stepping out of the darkness. Lala stepped up, gun pointed, ready for battle. When KK and Nene and Steve appeared it caught me off guard but I quickly rebounded.

"So what we got here?" "Yea my peoples are here, now what bitches?"

"KK this has nothing to do with your team. This here is personal." KK stepped back and admired me. He seen I was built for war; seeing me holding my guns confirmed that I was what he needed and wanted by his side.

"We're not here to save that man, I just want to make sure everything goes right and he is neatly disposed of." Black eyez turned to fear. His body froze. KK had just sealed his coffin.

"Nene what's good? I thought I was apart of the team, the family. How ya'll goin to do a nigga like this?"

"Easy my nigga. We heard every word you spoke out your mouth about your kids."

Lala and me turned back to Black. "Now let's do what we came to do."

Lala pulled the ratchet from in her pants and a baggie.

"K-Ne don't let them do this, please." While that nigga begged for his life I reached in his pants, pulled his dick out and chopped it off. He howled like a wounded bitch. I stuck his dick in the baggie. Me and Lala raised our guns but before we could get a shot off two bullets hit Black in the back of his head. Everyone was lookin at one another. I knew first hand where them bullets came from and why nobody heard them. Black's eyez rolled to the back of his head; he was dead. When everybody turned ,standing there with their guns out was Lil Mama and Baby Girl. They had plotted to kill him after talking to me. There was no way he would take me away from them. They knew how to shoot their guns since their 7th birthday. I had given them black, nickel plated .45s as birthday presents.

I knew their father was in the game and you never knew who he crossed or who was jealous so I schooled them to carry guns and shooting early.

"Baby Girl, how you two know where I was?"

"We've been following you since we had the family talk and listening to you and god mommy conversations on the phone we couldn't let him take you away from us. You and Lala is all we got."

I grabbed my babies and held them tight. I had brought my babies too far in this game without even noticing it.

"Chyna, KK yelled, get them up outta here. My peoples will clean this up. Go before someone notices all the wips parked over here."

I turned to look KK in the eyez. "Thank you, I owe you."

The twins, Lala and me where gone. Seeing me like that hurt KK. To his heart, this bitch ass nigga had caused me pain and getting caught was not an option.

"Steve, you know what to do." "I got this head out. I'll meet up with you two when I'm done."

Chapter Thirteen

Lesson Thirteen: A Dick Can Be a Powerful Thing

Meka kept paging Smoky but wasn't getting any response. Could KK know? What if he did? Is Smoky dead? No it couldn't be or KK would have done me off already. As Meka started to relax her phone went off.

"Meka, why you keep paging me? You know I'm working. You trying to get us killed." "No Boo it's just that I was missin you. I'm sorry, I'll be more careful."

"It's alright. You ready for our little trip?" "Yes, we still going?"

"No doubt. I told KK I needed to go see my family so we out tonight."

"Smoky let's do this."

"Is that KK?"

"Yea be easy. It's good, I gotta go."

Meka was nervous but Smoky said everything was good. Meka relaxed and lit a blunt. Her mind was playing tricks on her. KK and her was ok. He never showed any change. He was still helping with the bills, calling on a regular. Yea, her and Smoky was safe, or so she thought. Just to cover her ass she called her girl Keisha to go over the story one more time. Keisha was Black's girl.

"Hey Keisha what you doin?"

"Nothing, paging Black's ass for the tenth time."

"He aint answer you yet?"

"No, I heard he laid up with that nasty chick Shaya."

"I thought he deaded her for Chyna."

"Me too but my peoples say he in there with her."

"What you goin to do?"

"You know me, if he not in tonight I'm ridin."

"Do it girl. What I called you for is to go over the story again."

"Meka who you think you fuckin with? I got you. You're goin to see your mom cause she sick and needs help with them bad ass grandkids."

"Good lookin Kesh I wish I could ride out with you on Shaya. That bitch is scandalous and needs to get her ass whipped."

"That's ok, I got something for that ass. Meka real talk let me holla at you. Are you sure you know what you doin?"

"Keisha Smoky the one. He loves me and I love him. I know it's fucked up but KK don't even touch me anymore. All he cares about is the hustle and his sister, when I talk to him it's like he's not even there. He pays me no attention. I think he's seeing someone too or he's thinking about it."

"I feel ya Meka. But you know if KK or Nene find out your ass is erased. Be real careful, that nigga got a team far and near."

"Copy, we won't be here anyway. First we headed to Viginia Beach for the weekend then we fly out to Cancun." "Just be on the look out."

"My nigga, Smoky this your last day for the week after you drop that package off in V.B. for me."

"Yes I need to be with my family."

"I hear you. Go ahead, head out. My man waiting for you."

"Good lookin, K. I'm gone. I'll see you in a week."

KK knew he would see his lying ass much sooner then Smoky thought and when he finished there would be no coming back for his or Meka lying asses. KK called his number 1 bitch Lady.

"He moving, I know I see him."

"Don't worry I'll call you with their location."

With that KK headed over to check on Chyna and the twins. Smoky jumped in his Mercedes wagon. He dropped Mario into the CD playing him and Meka song (I Can Feel Your Heart Calling). That's how Smoky felt, that Meka heart was calling him. Smoky never meant to fall for Meka, the boss's wife, but something about Meka kept Smoky coming back. She couldn't cook or talk for very long, but she still treated

Smoky with respect she attended to his needs, whatever they were. She waited up for him, keep him fly, even though he was getting money. Plus that gushy pussy stayed calling. Smoky knew that they would have to tell KK. That would have to wait his baby was waiting.

"Baby you ready?" "Yes, meet me on the corner of 116 and 1st Ave, just be careful."

"I'll be there in a few." Meka headed out the door. Before she got out good her house phone rang again. Thinking it could be Smoky she picked it up.

"Yes baby- it was KK. Baby what's up?"

"Nothing just wanted to hear your voice for the last time."

"That's sweet Boo. I'll be back next Tuesday."

"I know I won't see you off. You be a good girl."

"I'm half way out the door." "I'll let you go then."

Bitch really think I'm stupid, let her think it; we'll see her real soon. Meka put the phone on the receiver, never even thinking about what KK just said. She was to busy getting to Smoky. Meka hurried out the building, Lady watching. She hopped in a cab, headed to her man. Smoky was posted up on his Mercedes when Meka got out the cab.

"Damn Baby you look good - good enough to eat."

"Yes that will come later. Let's get outta here." Lady watched from her Lex.

She hated these two; they where playing with her heart. Lady meet KK and Nene. When she was at her worst she was paid to knock off this neighbor hood clown, but his girl changed her mind and warned him Lady was coming. Lady was set to pounce on her mark. When him and his team was laying and waiting. She entered the apartment from the fire escape, headed for the room when the lights came on. There they where, her intended target along with three other nigga's she didn't plan on seeing. Lady was trapped with no way out. Billy, her intended target, grabbed Lady by her hair, throwing her on the bed. Lady closed her eyez; she knew what was about to go down.

Lady was bad. She was Latin with long black hair a pair of 38DD, thick in the waist, round in the hips and she kept herself up. Her nails and feet always matched in polish. Billy pulled out her ponytail.

"This bitch is bad and she a killer. Not this time, we gonna kill that Latina ass."

Trey ripped the rest of her clothes off.

"Hmm her body something else."

"Whateva, Papi. If you're goin to kill me get it over with. Fear no liv here."

"You talking tough for someone out numbered."

"It ok, I see'd you niggas in hell." Billy went first. He sucked on her titties while he patted her on her kitty. This shit was turning Billy's sick ass on. Her pussy was fat. He loved big pussy. Trey followed, sucking on her other breast. June and Kevin laid back for now. Trey went down. He wanted to taste her.

"Go for it my nigga." Trey licked down to Lady's belly button, licking around it then in it. He knew this was turning her on. She parted her legs a little. He licked on top, smelling her kitty scent. His dick was getting rock hard. Trey parted her lips with his tongue. At first no response. This didn't hurt. Trey knew he was a kitty doctor. Ladies couldn't get enough of his tongue game. He went at it again; she couldn't resist this time. Trey was eating that kitty so good. She started moving her kitty all over his face.

"Eat that kitty nigga. Look at her she loving that shit. Make that kitty pop my nigga." Trey loved the audience; the more they cheered the more he devoured that kitty. Billy watched as his man kitty munched and stuck his dick in her mouth. Lady was so caught up she sucked Billy off while Trey ate her out. Before she could breath all four men where on her, taking turns eating that kitty, getting their dicks sucked. Billy started the train first, one in her ass, one in her kitty, and two dicks in her mouth. That wasn't the end to her nightmare. After everyone bust their nuts on Lady she laid there bruised and pussy torn out. Billy with his sick ass turned her over tide both her hands and feet together.

"You came to kill me? Right with these same hands don't worry, I'm not goin to cut them off but I'm goin to hurt them so you know not to fuck with Billy Mason again."

Billy took his fish hook knife and cut all of Lady nails out by the root, leaving her no finger nails down to the bone. Lady hollered for dear life; that's when her saviors would come. Nene was on her way down to her brother when she heard Lady scream. At first she started to ignore it but the scream was straight out of a horror movie. She called KK telling him to come upstairs quick. KK boogied upstairs thinking it was Nene in trouble. When he reached his sister he heard it to.

"Nene what that nigga Billy doin to that girl?"

"Don't know, I'm goin in." "That bastard makes me sick anyway."

KK kicked in the door with his gun in the air. Nene had the desert eagle off safety.

Billy came running to the front, gun drawn. KK hit him first. Billy fell back, landing on the couch. He was hit, not bad.

"Nene watch that man." KK headed to the back; he knew Billy ran with a crew; but they where long gone. When KK reached the room he lost his stomach. Lady was covered with blood; her nails and toes where gone. All that was left was flesh and bones. KK headed back to the living room and put two more bullets in Billy, one in each eyez. He was a sick fuck.

"Nene, get some towels and help me get her out of here." KK and Nene helped Lady recover. They paid for her operation on her hands along with her feet so to Lady anyone who fucked over her saviors deserved death. Smoky and Meka was goin to get it. Meka climb into the Mercedes headed for Virginia Beach. They played slow jams thinking about their trip.

"Smoky let me ask you something. Shoot. Do you ever think about KK finding out and what would happen if he did?"

"What you think? How could I not? I work for that man and know firsthand what he would do if he knew the truth. After this trip I'm step to him like a man and tell him." Meka loved Smoky even more at this moment. Not only was he taking her on a trip, he was willing to risk his life to be with her.

"I love you Smoky."

"I love you too Meka." The two lovers rode the rest of the way jamming to slow jams with Cheery Martinez on power 105.5. Reaching the Marriot the bell boy took there bags and escorted them to the top floor Penthouse. Meka was in owe. The penthouse was huge; it had a living room with a view of the entire beach, the bar was stocked, the bedroom was bigger than her apartment, and the sunken tub was out this world.

"Thank you baby, this had to coast you a grip. I love it."

"Don't worry ma, I'm stackin paper so it's your weekend. Wait to you see it from Cancun. Meka let me make this call to this nigga I have to drop this package off to.

Then we can do us until tomorrow." "Make it quick."

"Alright man tomorrow at 2pm, good talk to you tomorrow."

Smoky walked out the room rolled a blunt and poured a glass of Vodka while Meka took a candle lit bath. She was soaking when he entered.

"You need some help?"

"Yes. Can you wash my back?"

Smoky peeled his clothes off. Meka watched loving her man's body. He climb in sitting behind her. She laid back, feeling his dick in her back.

"Lady dialed KK, their checked in."

"Good I'm not too far, I'll be there in a few. Is your connect working?"

"Yes he let them up."

"Good. Stay put Lady, Meka yours, Smoky belongs to me."

Smoky poured Olay body wash on the sponge, washing Meka's breast. He licked his lips knowing he would be sucking em soon. He washed Meka slow and carefully. She loved his touch. She spread her legs over the side of the tub so he could get to her pearl. He washed that area over and over. Meka was feeling it.

"Don't stop Boo I'm goin to cum for you."

"Cum for your man baby." Smoky keep washing in circular motion.

"Right there, don't stop, keep it there. Like this?"

"Yes your girl about to do it.?"

"Let it go, let it go for me."

Meka closed her legs, locking his hand in place and climaxed all over her man"s hand. She opened her eyez to Smoky kissing her. They kissed slow and long. The bell boy let KK and Lady in the penthouse. KK went in; he heard moaning in the room. Him and Lady eased there way to the room. No one. Then Lady singled towards the bathroom. They crossed the room looking into the bathroom. Smoky was sitting on the top of the tub, Meka between his legs sucking his dick. KK smiled, not a nice one though Lady opened the door wider. Smoky opened his eyez, almost falling backwards. Meka knew her head game was serious, but not enough to make a nigga pass out.

"Daddy you ok?"

"He aight."

Meka's body turned the water ice cold. It was KK. Meka turned; there he was, KK and Lady. Someone she didn't know.

"So Smoky, this your family? I didn't know you got down like that. You know this is incense, right? Your kids can come out retarded and shit."

Smoky couldn't talk; he was caught with his dick in his boss's girl mouth, literally.

"Isn't anybody goin say hello or offer me a drink? KK was luving this. Meka you never suck my dick like that. Smoky taught you that shit."

"KK, why you here to show off your new girl over there?"

Lady smiled, removing her gloves.

"What the hell is that on your hands?"

"You'll soon find out."

"KK I'm sorry man I was goin to tell you when we got back. Me and Meka are in love. We never meant no disrespect, it just happened."

"Say no more, Smoky. I believe you, just like I believe you two are in love, so you two should be together."

"KK that's some real shit. I appreciate it."

"Don't thank me just yet." KK turned around, pulled out the .44 and put one in Smoky brain.

"NOOOO! Meka hollered."

Her baby was dead, the one man who loved her dead because of her.

"Fuck you KK!"

As Meka jumped for his throat; that was a huge mistake. She slipped, hitting her head on the tub lading right next to Smoky. Lady climbed into check her pulse. It was faint but still there.

"So boss do you want anything?"

"Both there tongues with one swift of the nails." She had their tongues then she stuck them same nails into Meka's neck, hitting her major artery. Meka was dead for sure.

They cleaned up any mess they made and left leaving the two dead lovers KK and Lady headed back to Harlem with more work to put in.

"Lady, you located that nigga T yet?"

"No but I will. You know I would never let you down."

"I know but that nigga I want bad so get on it. He can't live to much longer as far as I'm concerned." With that Lady was on a mission, her mission find T and quick.

Chapter Fourteen

Lesson Fourteen: Scars Will Heal but Nightmares Are Forever.

"Roc Johnson Din: 105C23R0Y. You are being released today back into society. You'll be back, I know it, CO. Walker stated."

Roc just looked at him and whispered under his breath, "fuck you and this place."

CO, Walker let the inmates off at the Queens drop off center. When Roc walk out the building there was his girl J, all done up looking good, just the way he left her. J almost came in her pants when she seen her man. He had a bald head, a muscle chest and his baby brown eyez. To say he looked good was the truth, plus that walk was something too. J and Roc had meet by chance. Roc was getting ready to pull a jack move on this jewelry store in the diamond district. Chyna, Lala and J was buying earring when he saw the bitch Chyna, the woman who took everything away from him and had him out there stealing instead of stealing football passes on the green. He knew he couldn't get at her now so he came up with a better plan. Roc laid in the cut and watched as the women shopped, when they parted ways Roc made his move.

"What's up ma? Can you slow down for a minute?"

J turned, ready to go to war but what she sore was lovely. He stood 6'4, deep brown eyez, light brown skin, a massive chest and the most beautiful smile a man could have.

"May I help you?"

"Yes you can, let me be your man. My name's Roc, yours?"

"J." "Just J?" "Yes that's it."

"Do you got a minute?"

"Sorry I don't. I have to get ready for a party and meet my girls."

"Well can I at least get your number?"

J wrote her number down and was gone. Roc had it all planned down to the letter; he was gonna lay dick to J so good that she would tell everything on her girl Chyna so that I would be a easy target. Roc called J the next day to get his plan in motion.

"Hey sleepy head, you want to go to breakfast with me?"

"No. Sorry Roc I'm still tired. Can a girl holla at you later?"

"No problem. Hey why don't I bring you breakfast?" J thought that was nice.

"Why not? Here's my address."

"I know where you live."

"That's right, we meet in front of my building, remember?"

"Alright, here's my building number and apartment."

Ten minutes later Roc was there with L n T, special bacon, eggs home fries, and coffee.

J had taken a quick shower, brushed her teeth, changed into her sexy bra and panties under her long tee.

"Come in. That smells good."

"I know, let's eat in the living room, cool."

"J you got a man?" "No ridin solo. For now. how bout you?"

"Single. That's good, we both chilling."

They continued eating until J was full.

"Can I take that for you? Yes thank you."

J needed to leave the room; the heat between them was makin her moist.

J took his plate to the kitchen. Roc knew she was hot and followed her to the kitchen sink. He noticed her ass and her tits was sticking out her white tee. Roc walked up behind her, putting his dick on her ass. This made J hot as she washed the glasses. He placed kiss's on her neck. J laid her head back on his chest. Roc continued kissing her neck while his hands caressed her tits. J bit down on her bottom lip, feeling his touch. Roc pulled J's shirt over her head, exposing her body. J didn't move, afraid he would stop. Roc went back to massaging her body. Roc was now playing inside her panties; he traced the outside of her clit. J moaned breathing heavy, waiting for Roc to put his finger inside her. Roc took his thumb, flicking at her clit, making it rock hard. It felt good on his hands, first one finger sliding in and out then two, then three. He was finger fucking her crazy. J rode his fingers, leaning over the sink. She bounced and buck back on his fingers. "Oh shit that feels good, keep them in there."

"You sure you don't want me to take them out?"

"No! Fuck me."

"What you say?" "Fuck me."

Roc pulled out, licking his fingers. J was pissed.

"Why you stop? I was almost there."

"I know. I want that wet pussy on this dick."

Roc pulled his dick out moved J panties to the side and slid up in her. J leaned over the sink, then opened her legs so Roc could get up deep in there. Roc spread her ass cheeks with his hands to watch his dick slide in and out and banged her back loose.

"This pussy soaking wet, you sure you aint fucking no one?"

"No I said now shut up and fuck me."

Roc pushed J onto the wall, placed her hands above her head, bent his knees, placing his self under her ass and drove that dick in her.

"Fuck me nigga, fuck this ass."

J wiggled her ass, making it clap. This was rocking Roc; no one had ever threw the pussy on him like that. The two where fucking like dogs in heat. They were puttin sweat stains on the wall. Roc bit down on J's shoulder, grabbed her tit and pumped hard. In two hard drives he let loose all up in J. She cam sliding down on the kitchen wall.

"J that shit nasty."

"That dick mean too."

From there they where a couple. Roc sleeping over and them fucking until the sun came up.

"Roc, I want you to meet my girls Chyna and Lala today. Can you come over for dinner? They will be here."

He wanted me bad so he had to approach J carefully.

"J we need to talk."

"About what?"

"Your girls."

"You know them?"

"Yeah and no let me talk, then you can say what you feel. Back in the day we used to all go to Julia Richmond. I was the star football player. I had all the girls too. Everything was goin smooth until I decided to check Lala. Nobody was really feeling her so I thought I would bring her out her shell. We was good until that one day in the staircase. Lala and me was kissing, touching when she wanted me to fuck her. At first I was shock because she didn't look like that type but when she started sucking my dick I knew she was loose."

"What happen next?"

"After she suck me off we began fucking it was all good up until she turned around wanting it in the ass. I went for, it fucking her anal but the cunt started yelling."

"So what next?"

"Chyna was next. She caught us, walking up on me kicking me in my nuts twice. The bitch thought I was raping Lala when Lala wanted it. They ran, leaving me there. I finally made it up out of there, balls hurting and all."

"Ok why is that so bad? Lala didn't press charges or tell everybody you a rapist or anything."

"No, but that bitch Chyna told her cousin Joe and when I got back to school they had something for my ass. They had me walk through the lunchroom butt ass naked with a flower in my ass in front of the whole dam school. Everybody just laughed and dead smack in the front of the line was Chyna laughing her ass off. I knew she had to tell her cousin. I left Richmond, football career gone, pride down the drain.

I vowed Chyna would pay one day."

J's heart went out to her man. She was use to Chyna getting everything - money, car, men and anything she wanted. Right then and there J choose sides, Roc's side, without even asking her girls what happened. Now Roc was home with his boo.

"Hey baby give me some love. Damn you look good."

"Thanks baby, let's get home and get you out of them clothes."

Roc and J fucked until the wee hours, licking, suckin, biting - they baptize every room in J's apartment, ending up in the kitchen where it all started. Roc went upstate for attempted murder. He was out with J when this lame tried to get at her. When J refused his gesture he got mad and started calling J out her name so Roc put the steal to his dome, firing but J jumped in and the bullet hit him in lower stomach, causing the kid to shit in a bag for the rest of his life.

"So J, are we set to go?"

"No doubt baby I got you 100%. I know that bitch's every move but I came up with something better to make sure we trap that bitch."

"That's my girl always looking out for your man. Don't keep me in limbo. Let your man in."

"Not now Roc. All I want is some more of this."

Roc laid back, not wanting to disappoint and let J have at her lollipop, but Roc had another problem on his hands. Before he spotted J and them that day he had borrowed money from KK and promised to have it back in two weeks but that went out the window when he spotted his target. Now he was home forgetting the loan and plus his brother was dead, so getting the money from him was gone. The shit is KK hadn't forgot so he put a little man on the job to let him know when that nigga feet hit concrete. Roc didn't even know it; KK had him on lock also.

Chapter Fifteen

Lesson Fifteen: Hu$tle Hard Or Go Home.

I was laying in my bed with both my girls by my side and our guns on the night stand.

It had been one hell of a week. Lala and me plotted to kill Black all was goin well until KK showed up, and to make matters worse my daughters ended up killing their so called father. What was I doin? I was living a life of a single women ridin by herself when I had two girls that depended on me. Working at American Express should have been enough; I was pulling down six figures, I was in charge of a team that was killing the ad world, my cars was top of the line and I sported more names on my ass and feet than the law allowed. My girls stayed tough. They wore the latest shit. They even got exclusive shit. I had connects with Beyonce House of Darion. Me and Donna Karen was cool, her daughter did an ad with us so I was in with her and Kimora Lee. Let's just say we put her face on the card and she put my daughters in shit that never sold in retail stores, only in her Soho store, meaning the price was off the radar. Plus to end it all my mother Betty left me millions along with my fam Joe and Auntie L, God rest their souls. So by now you're saying why the fuck hustle? Why the fuck not? I was brought up by the best and that fast money was good money. My brother Mike moved my shit and Lala had customer on the smash in the Hilton Hotel. She was the manager there and all the business suits loved that white powder, the purer the better. The shit I was getting was the best. My worker Miguel

was a true prick but he had an uncle that brought that shit into the country and sold it to the highest bidder, except me. Miguel gave me my shit dirt cheap. You see, my cousin taught me every man has a weakness Miguel's was black women. He loved them, their walk, talk and look. His favorite was that split between their thighs. He would talk dirty to them and fuck them royally but by no means could he take one home. Miguel was Italian. They where not allowed into dark meat so he married in his race and crept on

the low. One day I caught him watching my ass during a team meeting; he was staring so hard I should have had two holes in my ass. When the meeting was over I asked Miguel to stay late.

"Miguel can you come in my office please?"

When he entered I was laying across my desk in my half stockings, high heels, matching lace bra and panties. Miguel's cock stood rock hard at the view.

"Miguel like what you see? He was drooling. Do you want to taste me?"

He nodded his head up and down like a little boy does when his mommy asks a question. I motioned for him to come to me and placed his hands on my breast. It was on from there. Miguel took over; he was pinching my nipples, licking my neck. He ran his tongue over my breast, making my nipples hard. He tickled my stomach with his tongue, landing kisses on my thighs. I opened my legs, letting him know where I wanted him to go. He took one look at Susie Q. He licked his lips, watching mine.

"Suck her for me."

Miguel did as he was told, playing with Susie Q between his teeth.

"I see you know how to eat pussy. Miguel put that Italian tongue on my pussy and eat it like you eat that pasta."

Before long I had Miguel sucking and slurping on my pussy juice. Miguel was eatin me so good I had lost count of how many times he made me cum.

I pulled him up to get that cock. I pulled out a condom and rolled it on his cock with my mouth. This turned him on; he was ready to fuck me. He bent me over my desk and fucked me right. That was the start of the office fucking until that fool put that white shit on my ass and sniffed it off. When I turned he had it all over his nose. I slapped the shit out of him and threw him out. Not to miss an opportunity, I propositioned Mr. Miguel if he'd hooked me up then he could keep his job benefits and all. He jumped on it so I had an inside connect. All I needed was clients, which wasn't hard to find once I got with Lala and Mike. We were making money hand over fists. My girls and me was eating. So Why did I keep making stupid moves when it came to men? First, Black's tired ass, then that situation with T and Shaya. What else could go wrong in my life? My bell ringing broke me out of my train of thought. It was my doormen George.

"Miss Chyna there's a Mister KK here to see you. How he find me and what was he doin here? Yes George let him up."

I slip out of the bed, leaving my girls sleep and closed my room door. I heard him knock. I went to open the door, checking my appearance in my full length mirror I had posted on the wall by my door. Damn I looked good rocking my Fredrick's of Hollywood black lace two piece pajamas set with matching thongs, hair rapped in a do bee, my toes was done up - I was good.

He knocked again, this time I was ready opening the door. There he stood, all 6 feet of him. He looked good, fresh goatee, low Cesar, beautiful hazel eyez, full kissable lips and that was just his face. He was rockin a Roca Wear sweat suit with a black wife beater and chucker's diamonds in his ear S. Carter watch and the platinum double cross.

"Can I come in?"

"Oh I'm sorry, come in."

"You look like you where in your own world."

"I'm sorry about that."

"No problem, Chyna. You doin it like this? Your condo straight out of a magazine." "Thanks I love it too. What brings you by? Better yet, how you know where I live?"

"KK knows everything on you, Miss, and I came to check on the twins like I said I would."

"That you did. They're sleeping right now. You want to come back later?"

KK wasn't there only for the twins; he wanted to see me and here I was flaunting my big beautiful body. KK could see right through my pajamas. I had breast that beg him to suck. They weren't too big or too small, just right, the way he liked them. My skin was smooth chocolate and my eyez was black as coal, looking into his heart. He wanted me but he had to come at me correct, no baggage, no middle man, just him.

"A penny for your thoughts."

"What?" "A penny for you thoughts now you're the one gone."

"No just thinking- thinking about what?"

"A lot of things, first being how you and the girls doin?"

"To tell you the truth I'm the one having nightmares. I know I had to dead that man but it keeps playing over in my head. Two shots then looking at my daughters holding the guns that killed their father - it's all so crazy. I'm having nightmares and them two acting like nothing happened. They hangout, talk to their friends, go to school like shit's fine." "Maybe for them it is. They took it as you or their father and they choose you so to them it's a done deal."

"KK I swear sometime I can feel it in the air, like someone out there to get me and I can't call it. All I got KK is them two girls. If something happened to them because of me I would die."

Seeing me upset like this made KK want to save me. He knew I was a hustling chick but he also knew I had a heart, a heart that beat for my girls.

"Hey C don't worry, ain't nobody goin to get at you or them girls or they would pay with their life four times over."

"Thanks KK but I can't have you go out like that for me and mine. You already did enough. And you have your own family and chick to look after."

"Don't mention that chick to me, and as far as asking me to guard you and yours, that's on me. You just worry about stopping those nightmares."

"That's easier said then done."

"Hey mommy what you doin?"

"When did you two get up?"

"About ten minutes ago. We hungry."

"I'll order something in a few. Say hello to KK."

"Hello KK."

"Hello ladies how you two doin?"

"We good. We want to say thank you for helping our mommy."

"Don't even mention it."

"Well goodnight, we goin in our room. Call us when the food get's here."

"Chyna, I got to go. Here's some money to get their food."

"KK I don't need your money to feed my babies."

"Why you so stubborn? Just take it."

"Do you want to fight me?"

"KK laughed. Na ma you have back up. I'm alone that's not a good move."

"Don't worry I won't call the girls, I'll kick your ass by myself."

KK noticed him and me was standing real close, too close for the both of us.

Before he knew it he was holding me. Feeling me against him made KK weak. He moved in for the kiss. Oh I didn't stop him. He placed his lips on mine. They felt good. He parted my lips with that tongue and searched my mouth. I let him. He felt good holding me. He smells like Sean John. He knew how to kiss. I liked that, not sloppy, he let me lead our tongues, made music of their own. This went on until his phone vibrating broke our hold. He answered it with a attitude.

"Hello?" They spoke for a few minutes then he hung up.

"Chyna I gotta go. If you need me just call me. I don't care what time or problem just call me."

"So if I call you'll just come running with both feet?"

We broke out laughing. I knew KK was serious.

"I got you KK. I'll keep what you said in mind."

I walked KK to the door.

"Chyna, everything's goin to be alright. KK here now."

"Yeah and where does Meka go from here?" "Dead."

"Goodnight KK. Goodnight Mrs. Chyna."

I closed the door behind him and there stood the twins with smiles on their faces. "Mommy why won't you get with KK? You know you feelin him."

"Yes I am but that's grown folks business so stay out of it. Now let's eat on Mr. KK."

I fed the girls and called Lala.

"What you doin?"

"Nothing much, just thinking about my girls."

"I feel you, I'm doin the same. The funny part you and I are goin retarded over this shit when they're not even stuntin the situation."

"What you think we should do?"

"To tell you the truth La I just spoke with KK and he said let it ride. If they're not trippin why should we? We'll keep a close eyez on them, not losing our minds over it."

"Good, now what's this about KK?"

"He came over to check on the girls like he said he would."

"Bitch who you think you talking to? You know that pussy skips a beat when KK around."

"Girl say that shit again my bitch soaking wet right now. If the girls was with you I would have said fuck Meka and rode her man's dick like it belong to me."

"I know that shit right so what happened?"

"Nothing really. We talked kissed then his phone rang breaking our kiss."

"So what's next?"

"Nothing. That's Meka man but he left his number. I'll sleep on it."

"Bitch just get it over with and give that man another a chance and sleep on him."

"You crazy Lala." "I do love him though. Ok sis I'm gone. Luv you."

"Luv U 4 Life."

Chapter Sixteen

Lesson Sixteen: Watch Your Back, Always look Behind You÷.

It was Friday I had just dropped the twins off at their godmother Lala's house. I was on my way home when J called. I hadn't spoke to her for a minute.

"Make it do what it do."

"I feel you ma, where you at?"

"I'm on my way home. Why?"

"Nothing special, just thought you like to hang out tonight."

"Sorry J, I'm feeling really tired and just want to climb into bed and relax."

"Say no more. Hey where my god children?"

"They're at Lala's house, why you ask?"

"Oh, I haven't seen them in a minute."

"Who fault is that? J, I have a question for you - why did you ask my girls who they would want to be with if me or Lala was gone?"

"I-I-I was just maken sure they would be ok living with me and not their punk ass daddy." "That's cool and J. I'm sorry for what Black did to you - you didn't deserve that."

J was stuck. Chyna just wished her well. Could she be goin soft? No that bitch was frontin.

"I'm gone talk to you later."

Roc and J watched me drive off. They made sure I was gone before they made their move. J called Lala.

"What's up Lala?"

"Nothing, working."

"You still working?"

"Yeah but I'm leaving soon, me and my girls got some shopping to do."

"That's good I'll let you go then."

She at work, they're by themselves. "Let's move."

Roc and J entered the freight elevator to the top loft. Roc hung in the back. J stepped off first then signaled for Roc. He hid behind Lala's oil painting of the twins. When the girls heard the elevator they thought it was Lala so they came out all happy until they seen J. "Hey girls how you two doin? Come give your auntie J a hug."

"Bitch please. Baby Girl spit you're not our aunt. We don't even like you."

"Who you think you talking to? I will knock your ass out."

"Then where you goin to live? You know our mother will kill your ass for even mentioning touching her girls."

"We'll see about that."

"What the fuck you talking about, this?"

J pulled her gun and stuck it to LiL Mama's head. Baby Girl grew pissed seeing a gun to her sister's head. This brought the beast out but before she could get to her gun. Roc slapped her so hard she fell face first. Lil Mama vowed to kill them both when the opportunity presented itself. Seeing her sister lying there made her heart hurt.

"Get up bitch, I didn't hit you that hard, but if you talk slick out your mouth again. I will stick this Timb in your face."

"Roc, slow down it's not about them. It's their mother we want."

"Shut up J. They're apart of their mother; they go too."

"What? You never said that. You said they would be motherless."

"I changed my mind. You got the note? Yes."

"Good, leave it on the door so she don't miss it. Now we're goin to walk out of this building like a happy family and if anyone of you try anything I'll shoot the other one in her face, got it?"

"Yes we got it."

Roc walked out the building first then the twins along with J. They all hoped into J's car and was gone.

"KK what's up little soldier?"

"You know that nigga Roc you put me on?"

"Yeah. Well homeboy home and him and his girl just left that other chick's house with Chyan's twins and one of the twins had a busted lip."

KK knew that shit wasn't good.

"Yo little man, you still following them? Yes. Good, call me as soon as they land, do you feel me? As soon as they land."

"I got you KK."

"You did good little man."

It's just one of those days came blasting out my phone.

"Make it do what it do."

"Chyna did that bitch J call you? Yea what about it?"

"Nothing, just that I heard her man was home. We ain't seen her in almost two weeks and now she calls."

"I feel you Lala, she probably was getting her back broke by that nigga."

"That's another thing - we have never met him. What do that nigga look like? Who is he?"

"La, I can't answer that one. How about we drop by her house tomorrow and see who he is."

"Thanks I'm gone, I have a date with twins."

"Luv you Lala."

"I luv you too, C."

KK's phone rang again.

"Talk. This Lady, I found T. He laid up with some Spanish chick in the Bronx."

"Good, Nene and me on our way. Nene let's go. Lady found T."

They jumped in the double RR and over the bridge they went. 138 and St. Ann Nene pulled up beside Lady.

"Where that man at?"

"In building 2228 apt 12-J."

"Is there anyone in there with him?"

"Yes the chic just them two."

"Let's move. Lady, KK, Nene posted up on the building until someone came out .They entered. KK wanted T bad. He violated the women he loved, now he was about to get it. Lady knocked.

"Who is it? Lady. Who Lady?"

Cindy opened the door.

"Who the fuck are jou?"

"Lady grabbed her by the throat. Your worst nightmare."

T heard the commotion by the door and grab his gun. Lady pushed Cindy back inside the apartment looking for her target. T heard her coming, positioning himself to shoot, Lady rounded the corner to the first bedroom. One shot rang out. KK along with Nene ran to the back. Lady was hit, not bad. Nene let off a shot hitting T in the leg. She knew her brother wanted him so she missed on purpose.

"Nene, get Lady out of here and dead that bitch on your way out."

Nene did as she was told. She grabbed Lady, moving to the front. On her way out she grabbed a pillow, laid it over Cindy's face and her and Lady put two in her head. Done. KK kicked T's gun under the bed then sat on the bed while T lay bleeding.

"K what's this about? " I'm not touching your shit."

"Oh but you did. You touched Chyna and that's a no-no in my book."

"Chyna? What you talking about?"

"I'm talking about the date rape move you and Shaya pulled on my baby, all because Black fucked one of your broads."

"KK, it didn't go down like that. Shaya set that up. She was mad at Chyna for taking Black from her, causing her miscarriage. She wanted that girl not me."

"Well you sure had fun doin it. But tell me something, how did you get Chyna to go along with it?"

"Shaya gave me some X. I put that in her drink when she went to the bathroom. The rest is history."

"Hmm I got to go now. See you in hell."

"KK wait, I got something for you, if you let me live."

"Ok, it better be worth it."

"It is. That bitch Shaya, she planning on killing Chyna. She has it all planned out. She gunning for Chyna and she will stop at nothing to hurt her, even if it means killing the twins."

KK thought not another one, he should have killed Shaya that day. That was cool Nene will handle her.

"T you did good. Now say what's up to the boyz in hell for me."

"KK shot T right between his eyez then whispered, you got a little piece of heaven fucking my queen. Never again."

Lala pulled up to her loft. She had bags of goodies ready for a movie marathon with her girls. As she entered she noticed a note. It read:

> *Yeah Bitches ya'll thought ya'll got away with that stunt pulled on me in high school. Well payback's a Bitch and I have the Bitch's Twins. If she wants to see them alive she better be at the new S. Carter Hotel room 112 at midnight tonight or they're DEAD and by the way the name is ROC JOHNSON......*

The bags hit the floor. Lala couldn't believe what she was reading. Roc Johnson had Chyna's babies and it was all Lala fault. If she didn't meet him in the staircase that day here girls would be with her. Instead they where with a killer, a killer with revenge on his mind. Lala knew what she had to do but telling Chyna that Roc had her babies was the hardest thing she would ever do.

"What's up ma? Them girls giving you a hard time?"

"No, Chyna I need... Lala broke down."

"Lala what's wrong? Something wrong with my babies? Lala talk to me."

"C the girls been kidnapped."

"What? Lala what you saying? Where are my babies?"

"Roc has them. Roc? Who the hell is Roc?" Then it hit me. J's boyfriend has my girls. "Why and what for?"

"It's Roc Johnson from Richmond, the one who tried to anal rape me, the one your cousin pulled that major stunt on and I believe J is with him that's why she called you and I to make sure we were out and not around when they made their move." "How you know they have my babies?" "They left a note."

"What the note say?"

"It says for you to be at the S. Carter Hotel by midnight or the girls die."

"That gives us four hours to move. You know how we do."

"Say no more. I'm ready to die or die killing that nigga."

"I know ma but he got my babies. He has to die and that bitch J too."

Lala hung up, ready to do whatever it took to get my babies back alive. I had gone to war many times over for her and she was ready to do the same for me. J crossed the line. She sided with the enemy and touched my babies, but why? Why would she do it? I should have listened to my girls when they warned me about the cunt. That was fine because the plan I had for her there would be no coming back. Roc was a whole another story. That man had my girls and if I didn't show up they could meet the same fate Lala did back in school. I would die first before I let that nigga touch my girls. Joe always told me that a bitch ass nigga would make a stupid move without thinking and I was praying that's what that nigga Roc did. If he didn't team up with no one killing him and J would be easy but if he did then I guess I would go out guns blazin. I thought about calling on that man KK, but he had already done enough for me. No, it was up to Lala and me *SO WE WOULD MAKE IT DO WHAT IT DO....*

Chapter Seventeen

Lesson Seventeen: Leave No Bitch Or Nigga Standing!!!

Lala and I hung up, ready for war. That lame ass nigga done touched the two things that made my heart beat, the twins Baby Girl and Lil Mama. They're all I had and nobody would take them away. I placed a call to J confirming that bitch was in on it.

"What up J?"

"Hey Chyna."

"Listen J, I just wanted to know if you still wanted to hang out. I can't seem to fall a sleep."

"Can't, something came up. Maybe tomorrow."

"Say no more, I'll see you tomorrow. That bitch was in on it."

I jumped up getting dressed. Black cat suit, thigh high boots along with the whisper twins. I called Lala, letting her know J was in on it and she had to die. My girl Lala wanted that ass so I gave it to her. J didn't even know what was about to happen to her. Lala had some crazy shit for that ass.

"So C, how we doin this?"

"We're goin in early to check the exit so we know the quickest way to get the girls out." "What if he has people watching?"

"That's true, but you know I can spot a mark a mile away."

"Let's do it."

"Meet me there at 11, that way we have enough time to scope it out."

Lala hung up. When she heard a strange noise she went to the elevator to check it. As she made her way there Shaya jumped out, pinning Lala to the floor.

"Hello Chyna's bitch.. Where your girl at?"

Lala reached for Shaya's face. The bitch had so much grease on it. Lala nails just slid off. Shaya expected this and back handed Lala with the butt of her gun. Lala's eye busted open, gushing blood all down her face. Shaya had Lala. Lala couldn't move. She promise to kill Shaya if she made it out of this. Shaya was reading her mind.

"Don't even think about it, there's no way out. When I kill that bitch Chyna, you next. For now though I need your ass alive so just chill."

Keisha had been paging Black for three weeks now, still no answer. She got her crew together and headed for Shaya's house but when they got there Shaya was ridin out so they decided to follow her. Maybe she was goin to Black. I paced back and fourth in my girl's room. Did Roc touch them? Are they dead? So much shit ran through my mind I couldn't think clearly. Then it came to me: both my girls had phones, so I went against my better judgment and called. Baby Girl's phone ringing.

"Hello?" I could tell by the sound of her voice she wasn't alone.

"Baby Girl it's mommy, you two alright? Yes. Did he touch either of you?"

"No not yet."

"What you mean not yet?"

"Yea bitch, I got your precious girls, they look good too. Maybe I'll have to make them women tonight."

"Roc you touch my girls the shit I'll bring to you will have your mother screaming you faggot ass nigga."

"Fuck you bitch, bring it."

"Don't worry, I will."

I made up my mind he would die a real nasty death. My mind and body was ready. I hoped off the phone, grabbed the twins and headed for my destiny, whatever that may be. J sat there looking stupid. She had crossed the line. She took Chyna's girls. She new Chyna would kill anyone or anything that touched them and listening to Roc talk about sexing them made her sick. Was there more to the story then he told?

Why didn't she talk to her girls about it? It was too late now. Chyna was coming, along with Lala. The war was on. Baby Girl sat next to her sister while they where being watched by some fat nigga.

"Lil Mama. What? You still strapped? Yes-you? No, I put my shit in my book bag when ma dropped us off."

"Why you do that? Didn't ma tell you to keep it at all times?"

"Yes, that's not important now. What's important is ma on her way here and she made needs us so just stay cool so they don't frisk us."

"You know what ma and Lala always say, NLB, Never Look Back, so when they start shooting unload your gun."

"Say no more sis, that nigga Roc and J goin to feel my heat if it's the last thing I do." Here I was sittin in the parking lot of the hotel that held my heart. Where the fuck is Lala? I was sure she'd beat me here. Let me call.

"Hello Lala - Lala what's wrong, you sound funny. What's the matter?"

"Nothing. What you mean nothing, why you still home?"

"NLB-NLB Lala what's goin on?"

"What's goin on is I got your girl, bitch."

"Who's this?"

"This Black woman the one you stole him from." "Shaya!"

"That's me."

"Put my girl on the phone."

"Fuck your girl. It's you I want."

"Yea the way you ate this pussy I guess you do want me."

"Miss me with that shit? Bitch I didn't like that stink pussy anyway."

"Humph, tell me anything, from what I remember you ate me the longest so your breath should smell real good. Ahh, the cat got your tongue."

"No slut, but you better be here in the next 15 minutes or your bitch here is dead."

"Do what you have to do. But know when I finish putten my girl to rest I'm coming for you, so think long and hard. Shaya, you dead my girl and I'm going to kill your fat stink ass, now put Lala back on the phone."

"Here, say goodbye."

"Lala." "I love you but my girls come first."

"Say no more. Make it do what it do and tell my girls I love them and C, NLB. We had a good run." With that I hung up.

My world was coming apart. My daughters were being held by some dumb ass nigga and his bitch, my so-called friend. Now Lala was about to die over a nigga we killed already. What next?

"Joe I know we haven't talk much but please help me. I need that talk. I need you right now, please help."

Keisha that bitch taking too, long let's ride on her."

"Let's get up in there."

Keisha and her girls ran on the building. Some took the stairs and the rest took the elevator. As the elevator came to a stop Shaya thought her prays was answered. That bitch Chyna had come. Shaya raised her gun ready to kill. When the elevator opened Shaya fire two shots hitting one of Keisha's girls. Keisha fired back, catching Shaya in her stomach. Rene rounded the stairs, firing too. She hit Shaya too, this time in her leg. Shaya fell, landing on Lala. Keisha ran up on Shaya, gun drown.

"What the fuck is goin on here?"

Shaya was holding her stomach. Lala thought quick.

"Keisha, this bitch here killed your man and came to kill me along with Chyna cause we found out."

"Your lying?"

"No I'm not. Check my kitchen freezer. She put Black's dick in my freezer to frame us." "Rene go check that shit out. If you lying Lala you next to die."

"Say no more ma."

Rene screamed. It was true, Black's dick was in the freezer in a baggie. Keisha ran in the kitchen. It was Black dick, she had sucked that dick on many of nights. Keisha came back and leaned over Shaya.

"You stupid bitch, you killed my man, my unborn child's farther."

Shay tried to speak but blood kept coming up.

"Keisha put that chick to sleep, one in the heart, Shaya dead."

Rene untied Lala.

"Lala we sorry."

"It's ok, but I have to go. It was ten minutes to twelve. Keisha, I'm sorry, that man Black didn't deserve to die like that but ya'll need to get up out of here and take that piece of shit with ya'll."

"Thanks Lala, we gone."

"Good I have to go, let yourself out."

Roc sat in the other room, waiting on his prey. He had so much wanted to kill Chyna, now he was finally goin to get the chance, but he had plans for her. He would fuck her in front of her girls, then fuck them in front of their mother, all anal of course. This would give him the final satisfaction of seeing that bitch beg for her life. Roc would be the victor in the end.

"Roc, what you thinking about?"

"Nothing, why?"

"Because you have this monster look on your face that's why."

"J what's up with you? Ever since we took them two little sluts you been acting funny, you change your mind? You not ridin with your man no more?"

"No it's not that, you just been acting real scary and now you talking about fuckin them babies, that's not what we agreed to. Those girls just babies."

"J get this, them girls are apart of their mother. She got me fucked up and embarrassed me all because I fucked her girl in her ass so they will meet the same fate that their mother will only after I finish with her."

"What you mean by that exactly?"

"What I said. Chyna is goin to experience ass fuckin at its best. I'm goin to tear her a new asshole, got it? And if you don't shut the fuck up with all this scary shit you'll be next."

J knew he meant it so she left him alone. She had learned the truth, Roc raped Lala. Chyna saved her but it was to late to ask for forgiveness; she was caught. Lala raced toward the hotel. She was an half hour away. If she could make it there by 12:20 she could help her girl out or she could at least get to the twins if all else failed they would be safe with Lala if their mother died. Lala was hell bent on killing J, if no one else. That slut would die for sure. She knew in her heart J started to change but not to this extent to plot and kidnap Baby Girl and Lil Mama. That was her worst mistake. She knew if nothing else Chyna or me would kill her so there was no turning back for Lala, however late she was she was goin to the hotel to kill J and bring back her family, all three whatever it took. Lala would make it do what it do. I climb off the elevator, staring down the hall, looking at the room that held my babies. A bunch of shit ran through my mind. Would I see my babies alive again? Are they dead already? Did that mark touch them? Did J watch and not help them? What- what - what is all I came up with. No matter what I was goin to get my girls or die trying. I thought about how they came into this world and they may leave ugly, all due to some nigga hell bent on revenge for something that happened years ago. Now is not the time to get soft. My girls needed me and I was goin to get them out. As I made my way down the hall his voice came to me.

Joe had come, get ready Chyna. A true female hustler is what you are, it's in your blood. Take no prisoners, leave no one standing, we got you. Me, Auntie L and your mother Betty. I knew they wouldn't let me down. I stuck my hands in my coat to check the twins; they where hot and needed cooling off. I was so caught up I never heard the hotel room door open behind me. Someone grabbed me. They covered my mouth, held my hands behind my back. I was being dragged into the room..........